©2012
Murmu

(Bool

Fifty Shades of Beige:

A Parody
10th Anniversary Edition

By Reid Mockery

www.reidmockery.com

Also by Reid Mockery
Fourth Wing Parody: Fifth Wing
The Housemaid Parody: The Horsemaid
Where The Crawdads Sh*t
Divergent Parody: Detergent
Fifty Shades of Beige Trilogy
The Fault is All Yours

INTRODUCTION

This is a parody of the wildly popular series of books by EL James. It is not a book for readers who are easily offended. This work, just like the actual book, includes heavy doses of profanity and contains descriptive sexual situations and scenes that are hilarious but also, at times, disturbing. The acts portrayed in this work are not meant to be performed on any other human. So, if you do and hurt yourself or someone else, you are simply an idiot, and this author or publisher is NOT responsible for your ailment or demise.

This is one of the first parodies to be published mocking the Fifty Shades Trilogy. I am sure many will follow, but I hope I have set a high bar for both silliness and humor regarding these truly mystifying books. I mean no offense to any reader. But, seriously? Did you really enjoy these books? Or were you just titillated by reading something that was more erotic than you were used to? We all know the answer. Wink.

Reid Mockery is a writer who is too embarrassed to write about such erotica publicly. But I am unafraid to poke fun and cash in on someone else's coattails. I apologize for some errors; they are being corrected, so skim over them. That's what I did in Fifty Shades of Grey—mostly skimmed over it except for the sex scenes (like you didn't). It won't hurt my feelings if you do the same, so I have noted the hot scenes in the contents. But, for the most part, sit back and enjoy the ride. Then, when you are done, tell someone else about this cheap book and post a review on Amazon. It can't be as bad as the mixed reviews for the real

Fifty Shades, so give me your best shot. I will read them because I don't have a life unlike EL James.

    Sincerely,
    Reid Mockery

    If you have comments, suggestions, corrections, complaints, or funny sex acts you would like me to add to the work, please send them to reidmockery@gmail.com.

Chapter 1

Beige Enterprises is headquartered in one of the finest buildings I have ever seen. I like to describe things through my eyes, and since I haven't seen or done much my entire life, many things pop into my mind as being the best I've ever seen.

I shouldn't be here at all. My friend Tease (pronounced Teeze) is too ill to do her news interview with this executive and begged me to do it. I'm not a journalist. I don't even know how to do an interview. I want to be a teacher so I can be underappreciated and underpaid. But here I am, walking into this glass monstrosity of wasted money to record an interview with one of Pittsburgh's most successful young entrepreneurs. A buxom receptionist at the main desk in the lobby greets me.

"Welcome to Beige Enterprises," she says with a fake grin. "How can I help you?"

"I'm here on behalf of Tease McGroin and Pittsburgh College. I have an appointment with Mr. Beige."

She punches a button and speaks into a tiny headset mic. "I have a young lady here to see Mr. Beige," she whispers. "Yes. She's quite attractive…I don't know…she didn't say."

She looks over the desk and examines me, and I hear her whisper, "About a 34 chest and 24 waist."

What the fuck?

She punches another button and then smiles at me, "Down that hallway to the last elevator. Go to the 27th floor. He's expecting you."

That was strange. I give her one of my oddest glares and proceed to the elevators. When I exit on the 27th floor, two attractive women with huge breasts greet me. They are wearing tight-knit sweaters, and from the looks of things, they keep the air conditioning cranked up around here. I'm no mathematical whiz, but I'm sensing a pattern at Beige Enterprises.

"Hello, Miss McGroin."

"I'm not Miss McGroin. She is ill. My name is Annis. I'm here to interview her." They look at me with puzzled eyes. "See. I brought my recorder."

"Oh, I see," one of the blond women says. The other one goes immediately to the phone and starts whispering into her headset.

"What is your last name?"

"Thesia. Annis Thesia."

"Have a seat. Mr. Beige will see you in a moment."

The view from this office is impressive. Too bad it's Pittsburgh and not some ocean vista or downtown skyline. I notice a landfill and a steel plant pumping out large amounts of environment-killing smoke below. There is a barge of garbage making its way down the river. I bet if I were outside, I could smell its sweet aroma. I can't tell if it's the Allegheny, Ohio, or Monongahela, but who gives a shit? It's a river.

A tall, handsome Hispanic gentleman emerges from Beige's office. He turns back and yells inside, "Cornhole this weekend, Beige? You in? Regular foursome."

Ahhh. So he plays cornhole—the game of champions. My parents could never afford the lumber required to get into cornhole. It was a game for the rich with custom-made beanbags and hoity-toity attitudes. Shuttup, Annis. Get your act together.

Some finance-related magazines are on the coffee table in front of my soft sofa. Two have pictures of Robert Beige on the cover. He's smoking a considerable cigar in one of them. Yuck. Robert Beige. Bobby Beige. B, B, Bobby Beige.

"Mr. Beige will see you now," the receptionist says.

Okay. Let's get this over with. I walk into an office the size of an average parking lot, and the walls are painted a light beige. The couches are beige, and the carpet is plush and beige. Mr. Beige sits behind a vast, dark wooden desk, pecking away at his keyboard. His right hand is holding a magic marker, twirling it between his fingers. The marker is beige as well. He looks up at me and stands up. The only thing that is not perfect about him is his necktie. It doesn't match his jacket. But, Oh. My. God. He is gorgeous.

Having locked in on his blue eyes, I lose track of my path and bang full speed into a coffee table. "Shit!"

Pain shoots up my shin to my brain, and I stumble down on his plush carpet, grabbing my leg. On my way down, my face smashes against the arm of the sofa, causing stars to pop in my head.

Beige slowly walks over and leans down to examine my status. "Are you okay, Grace?"

"My name is Annis."

"I was making a joke," he says, helping me sit on the sofa. "Your leg appears to be bleeding. Let me get you something. Blood is one of the most stubborn of stains for any carpet."

Oh, how nice. He equates my injury to the future value of his beloved carpet. Prick. As he walks across the room to get a napkin off his bar, I notice inside his pants is one of the roundest, most luscious asses I have ever seen on a man. Is he from Brazil? Just watching it shake back and forth momentarily makes me forget my name.

"Would you like a drink, Annis?" he asks. He pronounces it "a niece."

"It couldn't hurt. Thank you."

He pours me something, and I don't care what it is as long as it contains alcohol. He returns and hands me the drink and the napkin for my shin.

"Is it painful?"

"A bit. But I'll be alright." The drink is strong and burns my throat.

"Pain is not all bad. It lets us know we are alive."

I'm now staring at his eyes and every part of his face. He is perfect. His skin is just the right touch of bronze color. His hair is styled like a supermodel, and I would love to see him out of that suit jacket. I would love to see him out of all those expensive threads covering his...

"So, you are from the Pittsburgh College? The Ivy League of Community Colleges, is it not?" He pops the small top of the marker and slowly rubs it under his nose, inhaling softly.

"Yes, although I'm unsure where they got that nickname."

"How do you know Miss McGroin?"

"She is my roommate. She is sick and apologizes for not being here, but she wrote down some questions for me, and I brought a recorder. Do you mind if I turn it on?"

"Of course. Things work so much better when they are turned on. Don't you agree?"

What the hell?

"Indeed they do. Now, let's get to the questions. Here we go. Question one. Do you think size matters in business?"

He looks at me and raises his left eyebrow before answering. "In many ways, size can be an advantage. It can help you reach certain locations that would otherwise not be available. This business started small. But through tremendous effort, we could grow...and grow...and grow...until we reached full size. That's when we decided to erect this building."

I could have sworn his hips moved forward just a little each time he said the word "grow." I wipe my forehead and am surprised at how much I am perspiring. It's time for another drink. It goes down harshly and makes me squint, but I can relax.

"I see. Next question. Do you think you may peak prematurely being such a young company?"

What the hell kind of questions are these, Tease?

"While...that may be a problem for many...young...companies. I assure you, we are prepared to take our time and make sure all the needs of our...stockholders...are met before we...peak...as you say."

I take another drink. He looks straight into my eyes. I look down at his right leg, which is crossed on his left. His foot dangles up and down as if to say, "Come on over and sit with me. Better yet, sit on me."

"Miss Thesia?"

Even the way he pronounces my last name is sexual. He says, "Theezia" and draws it out like a foreign name.

"Yes?"

"I fear the fall has perhaps harmed you more than you let on. You seem out of sorts."

"No. I'm okay. Really. Next question. Your company recently acquired drilling rights for environmentalists who want protected lands. How do you plan to address their concerns?"

Finally, a typical question.

"When Beige Enterprises finds a place we want to drill, we take our time and go to great means to prepare it. We groom and lubricate it so the drill can be inserted properly without damaging the surroundings. When it goes in, it goes...deep. And, with our tender care, we pump until that oil spills out all over the ground. It's a glorious site to behold."

After an uncomfortable pause, I say, "You clean it up?"

"Clean what up?"

"The oil. All the oil on...the ground?"

"Oh, yes. We have special towels for that. I'd do it myself but I'm usually too tired after the drilling." He sniffs at his marker again. His eyes slowly close as he takes in the scent. I swallow hard. His leg stops bobbing. Then it starts again. I'm staring at it. He knows I'm staring at it. This is some whacked-out shit going on in here. I can smell him, and I'm six feet away. He smells like...pleasure except for that marker.

"What are you studying at Pittsburgh College, Miss Thesia?"

"Um. Education. I want to teach someday."

"Really. What would you like to teach?"

"Kids. Teens. Whatever. These days, I want a job."

"Maybe you could teach me…someday?"

I look around the opulent office space. "I doubt there is anything I could teach you, Mr. Beige. You seem to be doing quite well."

He sees my eyes settle on a lighted cabinet with Pittsburgh Pirates memorabilia. "Do you like baseball, Miss Thesia?"

"I do. I've been a Pirates fan since I was young. It's a shame what they've done to that organization. Don't get me started. The owner doesn't have a clue how to run that team. He probably only wants it as a tax write-off."

He walks over and refills his drink. "Interesting. It makes me almost wish I hadn't bought the team."

What? "You own…the Pirates?"

He nods yes. "I certainly do. Although, the only real reason I own them is to give me a proper…tax write-off."

Smartass. He's so smug with all his fancy clothes, fancy office, and creased pants hanging from his waist just right. I would do him right here, right now.

"Can you tell me why you continue to let them suck?"

He strolls back and sits on his overly expensive couch. He slowly crosses his legs and sips his drink. "Perhaps…I like things that suck."

At that moment, I realize I will have to change my panties when I get home.

Chapter 2

Tease stands up as soon as I enter our apartment. "What took you so long? I got worried."

"You said do the interview. I did the interview. It's done."

"So, what was he like? Robert Beige? Was he as good-looking as some of his pictures?"

"Probably more so. He is very charming and very weird."

"RRRRealllly? Tell me. Tell me."

"There's not much to tell. I went in, banged my leg on a table, and then I turned on the recorder. By the way, what the hell kind of questions were those?"

"What do you mean?"

"I mean, every one of them turned out to be some sort of sexual innuendo that made me very uncomfortable."

"No, they're not. Let me listen."

Thirty minutes go by as Tease listens to every word. I take a shower and change my panties. Just thinking about Beige's eyes and that juicy butt of his made me all moist downstairs, and it feels good to be cleaned up and refreshed.

When I come back to the living room, Tease is standing there, just staring at me.

"What?"

"He was totally flirting with you."

"No, he wasn't. Why do you think that?"

"Because I'm a whore, and I know when a man wants to fuck. He wants to fuck, bad."

"No. Really? I don't think so. He's not in my league."

"That may be, but there is no denying the tape. His voice—oh my god—it oozes sensuality, doesn't it?"

"Maybe. I suppose."

"Let's listen to it again. Just hearing him makes me horny."

It doesn't take much for Tease to get horny. She's beautiful, outgoing, drinks like a fish, and gets any man who so much as looks at her. I, on the other hand, keep to myself. I wanted to save my virginity for when I got married and found the right man to love. Now, I'm thinking that was a poor idea.

I need to get laid and see what all the fuss is about.

According to Tease, it's an out-of-this-world experience. I'd bet it would be with Bobby Beige. I've never had a man stir these kinds of desires in me like he did today. I keep repeating my name the way he pronounced it. A Neece Theezia. A Neece... Theeeezia.

It was so sexy.

A knock at the door makes Tease perk up. She swings it open, and Dumas enters with a wide grin.

"Hey, ladies!" he says in his usual dramatic flair. He raises his right hand and places his left over his heart. "In the words of the poet, Pink: Let's get the party started!"

"Woo-hoo!" Tease shouts, grabbing the wine bottles from his hands.

Dumas turns to me. "Hey, Annis. How you doing, girl?"

"I'm okay. I'm ready for the semester to be over."

"She got hit on by a rich executive today," Tease calls out from the kitchen.

Dumas' eyebrows shoot up. "Really? Pray tell? I'm jealous. Annis, you are destined for me. You know how I feel about you, girl."

"It was nothing," I say quickly. "Tease made me go. He said some things that she thinks were flirtatious."

"Like what?"

"Like, I'm rich, and I want to fuck you!" Tease shouts.

"That is flirtatious," Dumas says, nodding. "Bold and straightforward. Did it work on you? Because if you like that kind of talk, I can do it."

"He didn't say that."

"And who is this mystery man trying to woo you away from me?"

"Bobby Beige!" Tease yells.

Dumas freezes. "Bobby... Bobby Beige. The Bobby Beige?"

"The one and only Bobby Beige!" Tease continues, popping a cork.

Dumas whips out his iPad, tapping rapidly until an image of Bobby Beige fills the screen. "Wow. Look at those eyes."

"I know. And his lips. And his hair. He's too perfect."

"I'm not into men, but I would do that in a heartbeat, ladies."

Tease and I exchange looks, rolling our eyes in unison.

As I stare at the picture on the screen, a tingly heat spreads through me. I want to see him again, but I don't know how that could ever happen. I slowly swipe through the images, my fingers grazing the screen as if I were actually touching him—scratching his nose, rubbing his chest, mussing his hair.

Unfortunately, there aren't any shots of him from behind.

I would love to take both hands and grab hold of that round, muscular—

"So! What are we going to watch tonight?" Dumas interrupts.

"What did you bring?" Tease asks, refilling her glass.

"Rent, Philadelphia, and In & Out with Kevin Kline. He's so funny."

Tease scoffs. "Could you be more gay, Dumas?"

"How many times do we have to go over this? I'm straight as an arrow. I just happen to have refined taste. Take all your judgment and just put it away, girl."

Thankfully, Dumas doesn't mind me continuing to play with his iPad. I pinch the screen, zooming in until Bobby Beige's eyes fill the entire high-resolution display.

I'm going to have to change my panties again.

Damn it.

Chapter 3

I've earned money to get through school working at Lowe's. It's nowhere near enough to cover tuition, but it helps with my rent and food. I've got one more full week here before possibly moving to Philadelphia with Tease. There seem to be quite a few teaching jobs opening up there, and I have an aunt who's a principal in the area.

Halfway through my shift, my heart nearly stops when I notice a shopper in the hardware aisle. He's pushing a cart, scanning the shelves. I want to turn around and walk the other way, but he sees me.

"Miss Thesia?"

"Mr. Beige. What on earth brings you to Lowe's?"

"Just because I'm rich, I never shop?"

"No, it's just... I'm surprised to see you here. We're not the closest Lowe's to your office."

"I was out driving and decided to pick up some things. I didn't know you worked here. It's great to see you again. How's the leg?"

He said it was great to see me. Now if he would just turn around and walk down the aisle so I could admire that glorious ass.

"Oh, it's fine." I'm such a klutz.

"Was your friend pleased with the interview?"

"Yes, yes, she was. Her only regret was that we didn't get a photo."

"If that's a problem, I have some time tomorrow morning."

Oh. I'd love to take pictures of that—his body, his face, his ass. I wonder if he'd face backward for the camera. Probably not.

"Really? She would love that. I'll call her and see. We have a friend who's a photographer. How can I touch you? I mean... get in touch with you?"

He smiles. I'm such a dork. My face turns red, and I cross my eyes. He stares at me, raises a brow, then reaches into his breast pocket and pulls out a business card.

"Here. This is my cell number. Let me know when and where, and I'll be there."

He hands me the card. It reads:

Robert "Bobby" Beige
President & CEO, Beige Enterprises
I'd like to fuck your brains out.

"Interesting card. Do you hand out a lot of these?"

"Only to those who deserve it, Miss Thesia."

Oh no. My panties again. I'm going to have to start wearing pads.

"Is there anything in particular you're looking for here?"

"Just a few household items."

"I can help you if you like."

"Sure, I'd like that very much. Do you think these wire ties could hold... let's say... a human's wrists together?"

"Oh, certainly. They're very strong."

"Good, good. I was looking at this duct tape, but I'm not sure it's strong enough for my needs."

"Well, we have electrical tape and other types of duct tape. This one's popular—it doesn't leave any residue."

"Ah. No residue. Residue can be so... nasty and hard to clean."

"It sure can."

After picking up a few more items, he asks to be led to the aisle with ropes and chains. He smells incredible. And those slacks—with that rear end, he'd never need a belt to hold them up. His white dress shirt is slightly unbuttoned, revealing just a hint of chest hair. He's so dreamy. My heart pounds as he tests several brands of rope, scratching them against his skin. I wonder if what he said on the card was true... or just a joke.

"I like a non-abrasive rope."

I nod in understanding. I mean, who doesn't like a non-abrasive rope? Wait, what?

"And I need one that will hold its knot. Do you have much experience with ropes, Miss Thesia?"

"Not much."

"I must say, that blue apron looks amazing on you. Though I'd much rather see you wearing... beige."

"Oh, this? It's standard. Nothing special." I cross my eyes.

"You know, I really wish you wouldn't do that when I'm nearby."

"What?"

"Cross those beautiful eyes of yours. It's very sexy."

I actually snort when I laugh. This guy is weird. But so good-looking. Just hearing him call me sexy brings my panty situation back to mind. What's wrong with me?

"Thanks. Will you be needing anything else?"

"Yes, but I won't find it here. I'll need a pet store. Please have your friend call me about the photo. Or, you could call me... anytime."

He pulls a magic marker out of his pocket. It's a different shade of beige than the one he had in his office the other day. He inhales the fumes, closes his eyes for a moment, then walks away. I stand there watching his ass move like a ballet. Time to go to the ladies' room.

When I get back to the apartment, Tease is at her laptop, working on the article about Bobby Beige.

"I ran into him at Lowe's today."

"You what?"

"Beige. He came into Lowe's. We talked." And he made my panties wet.

"What the hell is Robert Beige doing in a Lowe's? And in this part of town?"

I shrug and hand her the business card. "He said you can call him if you want to have a photo shoot in the morning."

She looks down at the card, her mouth dropping open. "He gave you his phone number?"

"Yes. Like I said, he's agreed to have his photo taken for your article."

"Annis! He wants to fuck you!"

"No, he doesn't."

"Did you read this? It says right here: I want to fuck your brains out! He handed it to you!"

"I don't think that's what he means. It's a joke."

Tease rolls her eyes. "What's it gonna take for you, girl? He's rich. He's attractive. He came all the way to East Pittsburgh to your Lowe's. Rich people don't even drive through East Pittsburgh, much less get out of their car! He wants you bad."

"You think? But I didn't even tell him where I worked. It was just a coincidence."

"He stalked you down like a bull in heat. We've got to call him. You're coming to the shoot."

"Why should I do that?" So you can see him again, idiot.

"I'll get Dumas to shoot it. Where can we do it? What's the nicest hotel we have here?"

"The Hampton Inn Suites?"

"That's perfect. High class too."

Ten minutes later, Tease has booked Dumas and the Hampton Inn. Her mind is racing.

"This is really gonna help the article. And it should be fun. You call him."

"What? No."

"C'mon. He gave you the number. You call him. Tell him when and where."

My heart quivers as I dial.

"Beige."

"Um, Mr. Beige. This is Annis."

"Ahhh, Miss Theeeesia. How pleasant it is to hear your voice."

There's movement in the background. Heavy breathing.

"Yes, well... um. We'll have a photographer ready at nine-thirty tomorrow morning if that's okay."

"Ohhh. Yes. Sounds fine. Where?"

"The Hampton Inn Suites in East Pittsburgh."

"No, but I'm sure I can find it. I'll see you at nine-thirty. Oh... yes."

I hear more rustling, groaning.

"Mr. Beige? Are you alright?"

Deep breath. "Yes, Annis. I'm wonderful. Beige out."

He hangs up.

Chapter 4

Dumas sets up his lights near the breakfast bar of the Hampton Inn. Thankfully, breakfast ended at nine, and we have the room to ourselves.

"I can use the window; it'll be fabulous," says Dumas. He's not only an artist but also a pretty decent amateur photographer. He has shot many things for Tease and has taken several nice shots of the two of us as well.

Beige arrives on time. Wow. He looks absolutely delicious—tight jeans, tight black t-shirt, and a beige sport jacket. Um. Um. Good. But once again, his tie doesn't really match. Who wears a tie with a t-shirt? His hair is magnificent, and I want to run my hands through it right now. We all inhale his sweet scent as he enters. Dumas turns, and his eyebrows both shoot straight up. Straight my ass.

"Ah, Mr. Beige!" Tease says. "So glad you agreed to come. I'm Tease McGroin, and this is Dumas Rodriguez. He will be our photographer for today. And, of course, you already know Annis."

He nods and shakes hands with everyone. Oh my. His touch is like an electric shock moving through my body. I feel the moisture moving toward my groin. It's good that I wore a pad today. My period isn't for another couple of weeks, but I figured this might happen.

"Where would you like me?" he asks.

Anywhere, anytime.

"We've got you set up over here by the window. On the... sofa," Dumas says with a stutter.

Beige takes a seat, smoothly crosses his legs, and stretches his arm out on the back of the sofa, just like that guy in Mad

Men. Dumas immediately starts taking pictures. The lights make a loud pop every time he clicks the shutter. As the photoshoot continues, Beige occasionally makes eye contact with me. He winks. Then, I notice that every time the lights pop, he is thrusting his midsection just a bit.

Pop, thrust. Pop, thrust. Pop, thrust.

"Is he doing what I think he's doing?" I whisper to Tease.

"Just shut up. Yes. Okay? Yes. He's sooooo hot."

Pop, thrust. Pop, thrust. Pop, thrust.

He catches us watching him, and it only makes him do it more. He moves his hand down and places it in his lap as if to say, Here I am, ladies.

Pop, Thrust! Pop, Thrust! Pop, Thrust!

His harder thrusts cause him to rise up off the couch about an inch or two.

"Okay, let's try another pose," Dumas says, wiping the sweat off his brow.

"How about this?" Beige says.

He turns and gets on all fours, positioning his ass toward the camera. Dumas prematurely pops his lights without even looking through the lens. Oh my. The scene is hauntingly familiar, but I can't place it until Beige turns his head back toward the camera and says, "Yeah, baby. Yeah."

He's doing Austin Powers.

When the shoot is done, we all thank Mr. Beige for taking the time to help us out.

"Annis? Would you be so kind as to join me for some brunch?"

Excuse me? What was that? Brunch? With me? In a house, with a mouse, here or there, anywhere?

"I...really have to help them with the equipment and give them a ride back to campus."

I glance over at Tease, and she is sliding her index finger in and out of a hole she created with her other hand. Did I mention

Tease is a bit of a whore?

"If they can take your car, Annis, I can take you back to campus in my Lexasssss."

The way he prolongs the last word is creepy but also very sexy.

"Go ahead, you two," Tease says. "Dumas and I can handle all this."

"Wonderful," Beige says. "After you, Annis."

He actually grabs my hand and escorts me to the car. Bobby Beige is holding my hand in public! I feel a tingling between my legs, and I am so glad I wore my pad today. Please control yourself, Annis. He's just a man. A rich, gorgeous man who happens to like you.

His Lexus has so many numbers on the back; it's like a combination. The license plate is custom and says…Momma's Boy. I don't get the reference. The car is obviously new by the smell, and the leather feels good on my tush and legs. He starts it up by pushing a button. It purrs like a kitten.

"You will have to help me out, Annis. I'm not familiar with this particular section of Pittsburgh. Where can we find an appropriate dining establishment for brunch?"

"Um. There's a Waffle House just down the road."

"Ah, it sounds delightful. Do they do brunch?"

"Um. Yeah. You can call it that."

When we enter and are seated, the look on Bobby Beige's face is priceless. He has obviously never been to a Waffle House in his life. We can actually see the kitchen staff cooking the food on the grills less than ten feet away. None of them are wearing gloves, and you can hear the grill give out a little hisssss as perspiration drips from the cook's forehead onto the cooking surface.

"Don't worry. It's not too expensive," I say with a grin, sliding over the laminated but still stained menu that doubles as a placemat.

Beige takes out his beige marker and starts twirling it

nervously between his fingers. In and out between those strong knuckles it glides as his eyes take in all the wonderment of this house of waffles.

The waitress steps over. She's heavyset and has her hair in a net. One of the teeth on the upper side of her mouth is missing. She has some dried waffle mix stuck to the small hairs on her forearm.

"Get'chur drinks?"

Beige looks at me as if she has spoken a foreign language.

"We'll have two coffees and two waffles. Plus, I'll have a side of hash browns."

"Cream n' suga?"

"Yes."

The waitress writes it down, steps back three steps, and then yells, "Waffle on two! Drop one in a ring!"

The cook repeats the order. Beige slowly takes a sip of the coffee and continues to look around at the people in the restaurant. "I'm guessing we won't be seeing a wine selection."

I shake my head no.

He's so pompous and arrogant. It's good for him to be here so he can think better of my apartment should he ever see it. Compared to Waffle House, my place is the Ritz.

"Watching them cook, I feel there should be a lard limit," he says nervously.

"Excuse me?"

"Never mind. You may understand later. Do you come here often?"

"I've dined here on several occasions."

"May I ask why?"

"Because I have a death wish," I say as I cross my eyes.

This makes him spit out some of his coffee in laughter. Oddly, this is the first time I've seen him smile. His teeth are perfect and go right along with every other perfect thing about this man. Yes, he's arrogant. But look at him. I could give my virginity to an arrogant man.

"I have to tell you. When you cross your eyes, it is very sexy. You really shouldn't do it around me. I'm not the man for you."

"And how would you know what kind of man is right for me? We barely know each other."

"I know you are very beautiful. I know you are intoxicating. I've not stopped thinking about you since you came to my office."

He thinks I'm intoxicating! Holy crap!

"How long have you known this... Dumbass the photographer?"

"It's Dumas, silly. We've been friends since our freshmen year."

"You know he is very gay."

"He claims he is not. We've never seen him with any other men, but Tease and I have always suspected that he's gay. He displays all the..."

"The what? Stereotypes?"

"I wasn't going to say that."

He gently runs his hands through his hair. I want to dive in there with him with both hands.

"There is no need to lie to me, Annis. Our relationship should be based on truth. In all things. Many people have suspected me of being gay. I'm rich. I dress well. I have a fine knowledge of wine. Then, there is also the fact that I like to suck cock."

He sees my eyes widen and bursts out in laughter. The other people at the waffle house turn and look at us. I hope they didn't hear him say that. So, he has a sense of humor. I didn't see that coming.

"So, he is not your boyfriend?" he continues.

"Heavens no. But he does flirt with me often. How about you? Do you have a girlfriend?"

"If I did, I certainly wouldn't be in a place like this talking with the sexiest cross-eyed woman I have ever met."

"I'm not cross-eyed. I just like to do it." So I did it again.

"Stop it," he says, taking out his handkerchief.

I continue. This time with my tongue out.

"Please, you don't know what you are doing to me. I'm getting aroused."

I blush and decide to stop. Is he telling the truth? Could I have some sort of sensual control over him? It's nice.

"Let me ask you something, Annis. Will you join me for dinner tomorrow evening?"

"I don't know. I've still got one more week of school."

"But my Pirates are playing the red birds from Missouri, I think. It will be... fun."

"The Cardinals. St. Louis Cardinals."

"Yes. That's the team. I have a special suite at the stadium."

Owner's box seats at the Pirates? Hell yeah!

"That's very kind of you, Mr. Beige, but like I said, we hardly know each other."

Don't you dare quit now, you rich asshole. You better insist I go, or we're done. I may not be sophisticated, or wealthy, or even that good-looking, but I want to be chased.

"But what better way to make that become a reality? Please. Join me for a night of... baseball. I insist."

There was something about the way he said "baseball." He drew it out and made some sort of twitch with his tongue. He made it almost sound sexual. But baseball is NOT sexual. How the hell did he do that?

"Alright. Can we have dinner at the stadium?"

He makes a face but relents. "If you wish. But the thought of you eating a hot dog near my presence will cause me to lose some sleep tonight. I don't like to lose sleep."

"Okay, Mr. Beige. You're on."

"Please, call me Bobby."

They bring us our waffles, and when we are done, Beige looks over at me and asks, "Do you see a colon therapist on a regular basis?"

What? That's a bit too personal. Didn't see that one coming either.

"Excuse me?"

"You know? A colon therapist? A person that helps supervise the health and well-being of our intestines."

"I know what it means, Bobby. I'm just curious as to why you would ask such a question."

"Because I know for a fact I'll have to make an appointment to see my therapist after eating here. You should make an appointment as well."

"I don't think so."

"Have you any idea how many toxins reside in the average colon?"

I can't believe this is our conversation.

"Do you cleanse on a regular basis? If not, please consider it. I had headaches and no appetite. I always felt tired and exhausted, plus I was irritable all the time. But after consistent colon therapy, my life changed. I'm a new man. Seriously."

"That's... good to know."

That entire thing would have really turned me off if he hadn't just invited me to see a Pirates game from the owner's box. Woo hoo!

Chapter 5

He holds my hand as we weave through traffic toward the stadium. Bobby Beige is holding my hand! His skin is soft, and every now and then, he strokes the inside of my palm with his middle finger. It's subtle but undeniably erotic. Once again, I've chosen to wear extra wetness protection, just in case. So far, it's doing its job.

"I like your outfit," he says in that smooth, intoxicating voice.

"Oh, this?" I glance down at my outfit: skinny jeans, bright yellow spike heels, and my favorite Pirates T-shirt—a gift from my dad when I was twelve. It fits a little too snug now, so I cut it off to expose my midriff.

"Your stomach is sexy as hell," he murmurs. "The way it lops over your belt just a little? Very nice. Oh, and look at that—a tattoo."

I blush. "Yeah… I had too much to drink one night, and Tease talked me into it. It's a Japanese symbol. I don't know exactly what it means."

Bobby grins, looking out the window. "Oh, I do. It means 'please fuck me.'"

"No, it doesn't, silly. She told me it stood for peace or goodwill or something."

"She lied. I spent a year and a half in Japan, Miss Thesia. I speak the language fluently. That tattoo means you are desperate for sex. Whores in Tokyo have it on their ankles to signal potential customers."

Tease, you bitch. I bet she knew all along. How embarrassing. I'm going to kick her ass when we get back home.

We flash a special pass to the guards, and Bobby pulls the Lexus into the parking garage beneath the stadium. When we step out, he escorts me to an elevator. The moment the doors close, his scent fills the small space, and my body reacts immediately. He turns to me, eyes locked onto mine. I can't help it. I cross them.

"You don't want to do that in here," he warns. "I've told you what it does to me."

I uncross them and smile. His hand slides from mine to my lower back, resting on my hip. Oh, my. The elevator dings open, and the sound of an organ playing echoes from inside the stadium. This is so cool.

The owner's suite is empty. It could easily fit over a dozen people.

"Are we going to be the only ones here tonight?" I ask, walking to the edge to take in the breathtaking view. We are directly behind home plate, with radio and TV announcers in the boxes to our left and right.

"Yes, Miss Thesia. Just us tonight. Normally, I give the tickets to business clients, but I made an exception."

How romantic. A buffet sits under warmers, filled with ballpark favorites. A cooler of beer and several bottles of wine are neatly arranged. In the back, a display case holds an actual World Series trophy alongside baseballs and jerseys signed by legendary Pirates players. I'm so mesmerized by the autographs that I forget I'm on a date.

"This is great! How often do you come to the games?" I ask.

"I'll be honest with you, Annis. I don't care much for baseball. Yes, I own the team, but I hire people who know the game to run the business."

"So do you even know who these players are?" I gesture to the display case.

"I've heard of Roberto Clemente. That's about it. I told you—I'm not really into baseball."

"So what are you into, Mr. Beige?"

"You."

Not yet, sir. But it's looking promising.

We sit, and I dive into a bratwurst piled high with toppings. Bobby watches me eat with an intensity that borders on unsettling.

"Would you get me a beer?" I ask, my mouth full.

He nods, handing me an ice-cold Budweiser before pouring himself a glass of wine. He sits beside me but doesn't look at the field—only at me.

"What?" I ask, wiping juice from my chin.

"Nothing. Just keep doing what you're doing. Eat that hot dog. Eat it good."

"It's a brat. You know, like you."

"I don't get it."

"Bratwurst. They call them brats."

"That disgusting brown thing? That's a bratwurst? It certainly is the worst."

"Lighten up, Bobby. It's good. Try it."

"Maybe later, when I'm good and drunk. What's the score? Are we winning?"

"This is batting practice, dumbass. The game hasn't started yet."

Oh shit. What did I just do? I called him a dumbass. His eyes widen, and he stands.

"I'm sorry," I blurt out. "I didn't mean that."

"Oh, the truth is painful, Miss Thesia," he murmurs. "My mother used to say things like that. It was awful. She was awful. But I overcame her and became more successful than she could ever have dreamed."

"I'm so sorry, Bobby." I stand to comfort him. He buries his head against my chest, and I think I hear a quiet sniffle. He squeezes me tightly, then gently rubs his cheek against my breast. Hold on. What's that about?

Before I can stop him, my body betrays me. My nipples harden, and my heart pounds. But this isn't the time or place. It's a baseball game.

"I'm no good for you, Annis," he whispers. "You can do better."

"That's the second time you've said that, Bobby. You need to shut up and let me decide what's best for me."

"Yes, ma'am."

"Now, stop your whimpering and let's watch the game."

"If you think that's best."

The game plays on, and Bobby slowly starts understanding baseball. When it ends, he looks at me, proud.

"So, we lost, right?"

"Yep."

"And the score was 12 to 4?"

"That's right, Bobby. You're learning."

His phone rings. "Beige. Get Bobby Bango ready in ten minutes." He turns to me. "Annis, come spend the night at my place. I have a surprise for you."

His Lexus pulls into the east parking lot, and my mouth drops open.

"No way!"

He smiles. "Do you like to fly, Miss Thesia?"

A private blimp. *Holy. Shit.*

Chapter Six

Bobby Bango is all gassed up and ready, sir," the mechanic says.

Bobby places me in the co-pilot seat and buckles me in so tight it takes my breath away.

"Why so tight?"

"I want you to be safe, Annis. This is a powerful machine. But safety is always priority one."

I glance around, expecting a pilot, but there isn't one. Bobby straps himself into the seat beside me and starts pressing buttons.

"You're going to fly this thing?"

"Um... yes. It's just a blimp, Annis. I've been flying blimps since I was fourteen."

Who the hell learns to fly blimps? I should have used the bathroom earlier. All these straps are putting pressure on my bladder.

"Hold on. Bobby Bango is ready for takeoff."

We slowly lift off the ground. It's no more threatening than an elevator ride, but he still leans over to check my restraints. Soon, we're far above the stadium. The view is stunning. This is definitely a first—probably one of many to come tonight.

"So, where are we going, Captain?"

"I have a vacation home up near Punxsutawney. It's a special place. You'll like it."

"How fast does this thing go?"

"This airship cruises at a nice thirty-five miles an hour. My last one only did about twenty. This one is a speed demon."

Based on how far Punxsutawney is from Pittsburgh, I realize this is going to be a long-ass trip. I glance at the dash in front of him. There's a gauge displaying our altitude and a steering wheel labeled with directions: left, right, up, and down. I try to start a conversation, but all he does is lean forward, eyes locked on the gauges, occasionally glancing at the fans that propel us.

"So, is this one bigger than the Goodyear blimp?" I ask innocently.

"Fuck Goodyear! They don't know anything about blimping. Just because they scored a couple of sporting events a long time ago, people think they're the pinnacle of blimps! How can a tire company stake a rightful claim to dirigible aviation? Answer me that?"

Um, and who really gives a shit, Bobby? It's a fucking blimp. But I decide to play along rather than fuel this ridiculous conversation.

"Yeah, I know. Fuck Goodyear."

"Damn straight. Fuck Goodyear. Bobby Bango to base. Bobby Bango to base."

"Roger, Bango, this is base."

"Prepare landing lights at approximately 1,200 hours. We're currently cruising at 1,500 feet."

"Roger that, Bango. Please call us back when you're within fifteen minutes and we'll turn on the switch."

"Roger that, base. Beige out."

"You seem overly cautious," I say. "I'd like to take off these seatbelts."

"Blimp pilots are known for our safety record. Please keep your seatbelt fastened. We want to remain the safest form of aviation."

"But what would happen even if you lost both engines?"

"I hate to think about such things, but I would then pilot it like a balloon."

"A balloon?"

"Yes, my dear Miss Thesia. I would have to adjust the helium to allow us to drop altitude safely."

"So, we'd just float down?"

"It's not that simple—there could be gusts of—"

Before he can finish, I unsnap my harness and stand up to stretch. "You got a bathroom on this thing?"

"Please, Annis. I beg you. Sit back down and replace your safety harness. I worry for your health."

"I'm going to drop my panties and piss in the back if you don't have any options."

His mouth drops open. "In the back on the right. You'll find a small portable device for your need."

It was at that moment I realized I would do anything for Bobby Beige. Anytime. Anywhere.

A couple of hours later, we land in a remote Pennsylvania forest. The enormous log cabin, bathed in dramatic lighting, looks like something out of a wilderness fantasyland. Bobby takes forever securing the blimp before finally taking my hand and leading me along a rock walkway. The sky is clear, the stars breathtaking. They're aligned for me. This is the night.

"Before we go inside, Annis, I want you to know you don't have to do anything you don't wish to do."

"I know. It's okay. I don't do things I don't want to do. Except maybe go to the dentist. Or... eat at Taco Bell."

"Just because we're in a secluded area, with no reasonable means of escape, doesn't mean you're in any danger. You can trust me, Miss Thesia."

"I trust you."

"No, seriously. We're miles from anyone. There's no one to hear screams, gunshots, fireworks, barking dogs, or... shouts of pleasure."

"I get it."

Inside, the great room is three stories tall, dominated by a massive log fireplace. A moose head is mounted above the hearth. Bobby presses a button on the wall, and the fire flickers to life, soft music playing in the background. The entire place smells like logs. High near the ceiling, a wooden canoe hangs suspended—painted completely pink for some reason. The kitchen is sleek, filled with stainless steel appliances. If Bobby wasn't already attractive, this kitchen alone could get him laid by 75% of women in the country.

"Can I get you a drink?" he asks.

"Sure."

He pours a glass of wine. "This is a Beringer, 2012. White Zinfandel. It's sweet. Like you."

I'm not even a wine person, but I accept it anyway.

In the corner of the room is a large wooden instrument with mallets. "What is that?"

"Ah, my Marimba. Finest one made in the world."

"Do you play?"

"I love to... play," he says, raising an eyebrow.

"No, do you play the Marimba?"

"No, Annis. I have it simply to look at."

I laugh, but then he pulls out a folder. "I need you to sign this NDA before we continue our evening."

Holy shit. What have I gotten myself into?

I don't know, but if signing it gets him naked, I'll do it.

"Bobby, I don't discuss my personal life with anyone, anyway. I certainly wouldn't discuss this. Hand it here." I scribble my name at the bottom.

"And initial here... and here... and one more here at the bottom. And you're sure about this?"

"Yes. Now that I've signed it, does that mean we get to have sex?"

"I don't have sex, Miss Thesia. I fuck. And I fuck bizarrely. There is much more paperwork to be done, but for now, I'm ready to show you something. Come with me."

He fucks bizarrely? What does that mean? I've never heard

those three words put together like that. It's weird, but very hot. Just how bizarre are we talking, Mr. Beige? My knowledge of sex, in general, is a bit limited. Although I'm a virgin, I know his penis goes inside me once I'm aroused and lubricated, which, recently, has been pretty much all the time. Sperm is then emitted upon climax, and that's how my egg would be fertilized. But what's so bizarre about that?

He gently takes me by the hand and leads me to a wide hallway of logs. "This will be your room. It has its own private bath."

"Nice." It's decorated a bit like Cracker Barrel, but it looks cozy. He takes me further down the hallway and stops in front of a doorway.

"Before I show you this, I want you to open your mind."

"I'm open. I'm open."

"The last time we talked about it, you seemed a bit put off. I want you to take this with all my best intentions."

He slowly opens the door. Inside is one of the strangest chairs I've ever seen. The room has the smell of a medical office. What the hell?

"This is my colon hydrotherapy room. I hope that you will consider it as a regular form of treatment. Your intestinal tract can harbor parasites and pathogenic gut flora, causing sickness and general ill health. This kind of therapy has changed my life, Annis. I strongly recommend you consider it."

Again with the colon cleansing? Shit. Why won't he let that go? "Do I have to answer this now?"

"Certainly not. Come, let's go downstairs." He takes my hand again and leads me to an elevator. The door opens, and we step inside. He presses FRR, and we start going down.

"What's FRR?" I ask.

"My Fucking Rec Room," he mutters. "Before you see what you are about to see, I want you to know I will never hurt you, Annis. Do you trust me?"

"I wouldn't be here if I thought I was in danger, Bobby."

The door opens. He steps forward and hits some light switches.

Ho...ly...shit.

Chapter 7

We were standing in an underground cavern the size of an airplane hangar. Dramatic lighting shone down from the tall ceiling, illuminating a replica of a small town. I glanced over at Bobby, who was sniffing his marker as he observed my reaction.

The first building on my left had a sign that read "OBGYN Services." The next one, larger than the first, said "Costumes" above its door. My eyes moved around the space, landing on a leather goods store with sensually dressed mannequins in the windows. At the far end of the room, there was a stable, where a donkey, a sheep, and a goat were moving around. Beside it was an oriental massage and spa room that advertised "waxing."

Further on, there was a hotel decorated like it was from the 1800s. And finally, to my right was the largest room, labeled "Baby Supplies."

"Say something," Bobby said.

"How about, 'what the hell?'"

"Not entirely unexpected. This room is... unique."

"Unique? It's a small town! Who has a small town as their rec room?"

"Fucking rec room," he corrected. "It's for fucking. I told you I like to fuck in bizarre ways. This place affords me all possibilities. This, Annis, is where I will make you murmur."

"Murmur?"

"Yes, it's a sexual language. Murmuring. You'll know it when you do it."

Whatever. "Do you bring all your women here?"

"Not all. Not many, actually. I'm showing it to you because I desire you, Miss Thesia. I desire you more than you know. And I want to please you here and have you please me. Now that you've seen it with no staff, we can return upstairs to discuss it."

"No staff? What do you mean?"

"When I plan to use the room, I make arrangements and have it fully staffed with an actual OBGYN, real Asian spa specialists, shop owners, and my stable manager. All needs are supplied without having to go beyond the residence. Some of the role players are true professionals in every sense of the word. Others are just actors. Like the dwarfs."

The dwarfs?

He took me on a tour of each room. They were finely detailed and equipped with anything you could want. The doctor's office even had an actual defibrillator inside, and Bobby told me it was all very real. When we reached the stable, I noticed the absence of any of the usual smells associated with barn animals.

"I suppose you're wondering why there's no odor," he said. "Most women do. My veterinarian performs regular colonics on each of the animals. This reduces their..."

"I get it. But, why do you have these animals?"

"Should I remind you of the definition of bizarre, Annis? I'm open to all forms of sexual pleasure. Inter-species is but one."

He fucks goats. Holy shit. Bobby was a total whack job. But he was so handsome. Why would someone who looked like him ever want to have sex with anything other than a woman? I was really, really struggling with this right now. Part of me wanted to leave, but other parts—yeah, those parts—wanted me to stay and find out what Mr. Beige was really all about.

"I don't want to talk about this," I said. "Let's move on."

"All the options in this rec room are not for everyone. There are limits we will discuss upstairs."

We went through the hotel, and it was clear this was where most of the action took place. There was an S&M room, complete with whips, chains, and various sex toys. A video recording room with mirrors, cameras, and large video screens. Next to it was a room with an overly large baby crib, the size of a king-size bed.

There was a replica of a schoolroom with an out-of-place gerbil cage, a modern office, and a room simulating the interior of an airplane. Finally, on the top floor of the hotel, there was an exact duplicate of the bridge of the Enterprise.

"It's the bridge of the Enterprise," Bobby said.

"I don't know what that means," I said.

"You will. In time, my little Miss Uhura. I hope."

"Why are you showing me all this, Bobby?"

"Because I want you to enjoy it with me. All of it. You've cast a spell on me, Annis Thesia, and I'm weak in your presence."

Me? He wanted me?

"But Bobby, look at me. You are the most attractive man I've ever seen, much less known! Can you say that about me?"

"Um... no."

"You have everything. Money. Success. Intelligence. What do I have that could possibly interest you?"

"Those eyes, Annis. Those beautiful, big, brown..."

I crossed them.

"Oh, God. Don't do that here of all places. Let's go back upstairs."

My mind was spinning by the time we sat down in front of the fireplace. He brought me more wine and another piece of paper from a folder. I gulped down the entire glass, and he had to pour me a second.

"Like I said, Miss Thesia. There are rules. Here's a basic list you need to read, but if you have any questions, I'm more than happy to explain. These rules are part of a larger contract I want us to go over before the merger."

"The merger?"

"Of my penis and your vagina."

I blushed. Oh, that merger. Rules, schmools. Let's get on with this.

"The first page consists of many of the standard health questions you might be asked prior to any doctor's visit: allergies, prescription medications, STDs, and the like. The next page explains my expectations. I want you to become my dominant sexual partner. I will become your submissive partner. But although I will do anything you request, I am free to improvise suggestions. Please take the time to read these rules. I've got to make a few phone calls for my business. Take your time and sip your wine. Sip. Please don't gulp like a damn bullfrog."

He was right. I started reading.

RULES:
Obedience:
The Dominant (you) will discipline the Submissive (me) when instructions have been given but not followed. The form of discipline will be at the discretion of the Dominant and should be painful, equal to the level of disobedience displayed by the Submissive. The Submissive will engage in any sexual activity required by the Dominant with the exception of those items outlined in the Hard Limits section of Appendix 2.

Sleep:
The Dominant will be responsible for getting adequate amounts of sleep in order to properly discipline the Submissive. The Dominant will offer to sleep in the crib with the Submissive if that is deemed the only manner to get the Submissive to sleep.

Breastfeeding:
The Dominant will take regular hormone treatments to ensure the production of breast milk to provide to the Submissive. When the Submissive is not around to feed, the Dominant will use appropriate pump devices to save the milk for later use.

Colon Therapy:
The Dominant will participate with the Submissive in regular colon therapy sessions for a minimum of once per week.

Personal Hygiene/Beauty:
The Dominant will make all efforts to maintain her looks. This includes the use of beauticians and stylists provided by the

Submissive. Services provided as part of the agreement include but are not limited to: hair, skin, teeth, fingernails, toenails, makeup, nasal/ear canal, vaginal/anal canal, halitosis treatment, diet, muscle tone, body fat, body scent, cellulite, and pubic hair.

Personal Behavior:

The Dominant will not partake of the following for the length of the contract:

1. Chewing tobacco or dipping tobacco (snuff).
2. Vaginal piercings
3. Nascar telecasts or events
4. Mixed Martial Arts telecasts or events
5. Professional Wrestling telecasts or events
6. The Masked Singer
7. Domestic beer
8. Footwear known as flip flops (any flat sandals with a single thong toe hold)
9. Krystal or White Castle hamburgers
10. Any other man's penis, toes, fingers, tongue, nose, fists, or ears.

Gifts:

The Dominant will accept funds from the Submissive for purchases of acceptable gifts to make the Dominant more acceptable to the peer group and societies frequented by the Submissive (i.e., so the Dominant will no longer look like an East Pittsburgh trailer prostitute).

Failure to comply with any of these rules will result in the immediate termination of the relationship and Beige Enterprises will stop at no means to ruin your credit rating for the remainder of your lifetime. Beige Enterprises will also publish a picture of you with your last known address in Sex Offender's Weekly.

"Bobby, I really don't understand a lot of this."

"I'm sure you have lots of questions. Please feel free to ask me anything."

"I don't really know where to begin. Um... what's a hard limit?"

"These are things you will definitely not want to do. For instance... say... give the donkey a hand job."

"YES. That would be a good example!"

"Okay, fine. We'll put that in the contract if you wish as one of your hard limits. But, when it comes to that donkey, you may want to get really specific as to what you will not want to do."

"What do you mean by using a stylist to help with my pubic hair?"

"The pubic area is what I would refer to as a high traffic area. It has to be properly maintained for maximized pleasure. I don't want to be hocking up one of your hairs like it was some sort of popcorn kernel stuck in my throat. My Asian friends can help you with that."

"This stuff you plan to pay for. The makeover, the clothes? If the relationship ends, what will happen?"

"Then we will extract what is owed as a refund to be fair. Your teeth, your liposuction, your breast implants. Whatever. It all comes back."

"But, that makes this more like you are paying for sex."

"The Dominant/Submissive relationship is very much whore-based. It is part of the scenario we are going to be pleasuring ourselves. It is logical. Trust me."

"All this work to fix me? I thought you found me very desirable as I am?"

"That's true, Annis. But, look at yourself. You could use a tune-up, as they say in the auto world. But I will NEVER change those eyes."

"Breastfeeding? Really?"

"My particular affliction is called Autonepiophilia, also known as Infantalism. Part of the role of being the Dominant requires you to accept a motherly role with the Submissive. Breastfeeding is a very important aspect of this relationship. The hormone treatments will have no other effect on you other than your breasts. It is perfectly safe. Plus, I love breast milk. I have some in the refrigerator if you're interested."

"I'll pass."

"It is rich in nutrients. I think I'll have a glass."

"And who did you get that from? I thought you were single?"

"I have a case left over from my last relationship. It freezes and keeps. Now that you've read the rules, allow me to share with you my hard limits."

This should be interesting.

Hard Limits (For Submissive)

The following items shall not be shoved in the anal cavity of the Submissive:

1. Ball Pein Hammer
2. Shovel
3. Arms or Legs of any Dwarf
4. Any Living Snake
5. Bowling Ball
6. Parrot or Any Exotic Bird
7. Leaf Blower
8. Power Washer

There will be no sexual acts that involve voluntary vacating of bowels or bladder.

There will be no purposeful stoppage of the heart as a means of pleasure. No vomiting upon Submissive is allowed. No mocking of penis length, girth, form of circumcision, or color.

Why would he need to write these down unless he'd had a bad experience before? What the hell kind of freak was he? I'm alone in a cabin far out in the woods with a powerful man who has all sorts of bizarre sexual history. How hot is that?

"May I ask a personal question?"

"Sure, Annis. I'll answer anything."

"Why are you like this? It doesn't seem normal."

"Part of the reason is my childhood, I suppose. At least that's what my therapist says. It all goes back to that Catholic camping trip I took. My father served as our scoutmaster, and things got out of hand, so to speak. I was abused by several priests while my father watched and laughed."

"I'm so sorry, Bobby," I say, giving him a hug. "Sexual abuse is unforgivable."

"Oh, they didn't abuse me sexually. That would have been fine. They made me play something called tetherball. There was my father laughing and laughing as that ball went round and around that fucking pole." He takes out his marker and inhales deeply.

"And what's with the magic marker? Surely, you don't get high on those, do you?"

"You couldn't with any normal marker. But I have these made for me overseas. I have over fifty different shades of my favorite color. All custom. They're the only ones in the world. Take a whiff."

"No, really. I shouldn't."

He pulls out another one from his pocket and hands it to me. "You will like it. Trust me. Put it in your purse. It'll remind you of me."

I take it and instinctively begin twirling it between my fingers like he does. "Bobby, I have to tell you something."

"What is that?"

"I've... um... I've never had sex before."

"Excuse me?"

"Never. I've not had sex. With anyone. Ever."

He gulps. "You're shitting me? Seriously?"

"Never."

"C'mon. You've never done it. Not once?"

"I'm serious. I'm a virgin, okay? I didn't plan it. It just turned out that way."

"I just don't get it, Annis. You're very attractive in your own way. How could you avoid sex?"

"Don't get mad at me. I just haven't."

"I would have NEVER taken you to the Rec Room if I'd known about your inexperience. That's a place for... very advanced fuckery."

"Then, maybe... I need to be taught."

Bobby gets up and paces the room. I stare at his round behind. He is silent for nearly an entire minute. What is he going to say? I am inexperienced. I am out of his league. But, I want him to show me his bizarre, fucked-up marker-sniffing world.

"Well... I didn't expect this. Lesson one needs to begin."

Chapter 8

He escorts me to his library, a grand space with at least five thousand items stacked neatly on wooden shelves. Two giant reading chairs sit beside a coffee table, and another fireplace adds to the room's warmth. Bobby walks over to a computer and starts typing rapidly on the keyboard.

"What's that?" I ask.

"My library is organized with some advanced cataloging software. Organization is key to anything, Miss Thesia. You, as a future teacher, should understand that. Okay. Here we go. Shelf six, row four. A good place to start."

The library shelves are labeled with custom engraved brass numbers. As I scan the collection, I notice a significant portion is about sex—books, DVDs, instructional materials. Bobby slides his fingers down an aisle, locating the book he wants to show me.

"Sit down, Annis. Take a look at this." He hands me a picture book titled Mommy and Daddy are Having a Baby.

"Bobby! I know how sex works, I just haven't done it."

"Oh, sorry. My apologies. So, you are familiar with how the male penis becomes—"

"Yes. I know."

"Alright." He gently places the picture book back on the shelf, then returns to the computer, typing out more queries.

"Shelf three, row two. Try this one."

He hands me a hardcover volume entitled Chasing The Big O. It's at least five hundred pages, filled with graphic color photos.

"What's the big O?" I ask.

"Orgasm, Annis. Please tell me you have at least self-pleasured to orgasm?"

I cross my eyes at him.

"Oh my sweet, sweet, simple girl. The orgasm is what makes life worth living. Its lure has destroyed men, women, governments, countries, and one of the greatest golfers of all time. To go through life without it is to be unfulfilled as a human being. Once you experience it, you will dedicate and schedule your life to its pursuit. You will crave it, think about it constantly, and do all within your power to have more of them. It is the drug of drugs, and it's all inside you, waiting to burst out."

Oh my God. He's making me moist. I need to see what he's talking about. Have I truly missed out on one of life's greatest experiences?

"So, I take it you've had several?" I ask.

"By my last count, I have had just over twenty-five thousand of them."

Holy shit.

"So when did you start?"

"I believe at the age of five. And I average three a day. Sometimes more, sometimes less. But, I never miss an entire day. It's like an apple or a vitamin. But, as one of my rules, I will not self-pleasure during our contract, and I don't want you to either. We must save ourselves for the Rec Room. Trust me. It'll be worth the wait."

That won't be a problem.

"Okay, Miss Thesia. Now is the time to rectify your situation. It is time to Chase Your O." He takes me by the hand and leads me to my bedroom.

"Here? Not downstairs?"

"You are not ready for that, my sweet cross-eyed thing. Before you learn the pleasures of fucking bizarrely, you must start by knowing what it is to fuck normally."

That makes sense.

He places a hand behind my neck, and I hear his heart beating. His breath is fresh as his tongue plunges into my mouth, swirling around my teeth. It's so erotic. My body goes limp as he lays me down on the mattress. His length presses against me, and there's a strange bulge below his hip. Is that his—? Yes. It has to be.

Slowly, Bobby starts undoing the buttons on my blouse. He gets stuck on the third one and suddenly rips it off. "Dammit."

I slip off the blouse, and only my bra separates my breasts from Mr. Beige. He buries his mouth on my neck, licking and sucking. Oh my. That's good. He lifts me slightly to access the back clasps of my bra. He struggles, but soon it pops free. I am now topless before him. He leans back to inspect my body and softly whispers, "Oh, Momma."

He proceeds to suck my breasts so hard I think they might come off like the cap of a beer bottle. It feels good, yet hurts at the same time. He plays with my nipples, twirling them like adjusting a radio dial. He pushes them together and places his nose between them, making the gentle sounds of a small motorboat. Then, he presses his eyeballs to my nipples, as if looking through binoculars, twisting as if trying to find focus. He blinks his eyelashes, tickling my skin. Holy crap! He is so good at this.

My hands grope every part of him I can reach. He sits up, unbuttoning his dress shirt. His chest is bare and glistening in the dim light. His muscles are tight. I poke his pectorals, and there's no give. I keep poking, and he smiles.

"That's it, baby. Poke me anywhere you like," he murmurs.

I unbutton my skinny jeans, and he pulls them off my legs. My panties are next, and I totally forgot about my stupid pad. He looks at it, makes a face, but realizes there's no blood, so full speed ahead.

"Aha. The carpet matches the drapes," he says.

Oh, so that's what that means.

Then, his face is buried between my legs. Oh shit. I'm not shaved.

He likes women to be shaved. I'm pretty sure my pube line

starts two inches below my belly button and stretches to my outer hips. How do you even shave there? Forget it. Concentrate on what he's doing. I'm pretty sure that's his nose moving around my—

He turns his head sideways and sticks his ear inside me. In and out, in perfect rhythm. He's saying something, but I can't hear a word. His ear feels so good. No one has ever told me about this kind of sex.

He lifts my legs straight up at the ceiling. The nerves, my heart—what is he doing? Something is building inside me. He intertwines his fingers with my toes, massaging my feet. Holy cow. My hips thrust upward as he switches from ear to tongue. He starts to choke, but I don't stop. I want to pull his entire head inside me. My legs squeeze around him like a clamp.

"ANNUTH! STOPTH! ANNUTH!"

It's close—this must be it! Oh my God—

"AHHHHHHHHH!"

Every muscle in my body tingles. My eyes cross. I let out a queef along with other things. My breathing is heavy, and my head spins. That had to be the big O. Why have I gone all these years without that? I've awakened my inner slut.

Bobby regains composure, standing over my shivering body.

I can't speak. My heart pounds in my chest. Sweat clings to my skin. I need to clean myself up. But wow—was that something.

"So, Miss Thesia. You now know what an orgasm is and are no longer a virgin. How do you feel?"

"I feel a bit sore, to tell you the truth."

"You're welcome. Now, you need to go to sleep. I'll see you in the morning."

"Bobby?"

"Yes?"

"Thank you. You know...for..."

"The normal fuck, yes. I know. It's okay, Annis. Wait until

you experience the bizarre fuck. It will blow your mind."

Chapter 9

The next morning, I'm awakened by sounds in the kitchen. I slip on one of Bobby's T-shirts, the fabric soft against my skin, and step out to greet the day. Sunlight filters through the trees, casting golden beams onto the sleek surface of Bobby's blimp. It's fastened down on a large paved square, a giant white "B" painted in the center of a circle like a personal landing pad.

"Ah, there you are. I made breakfast. Have a seat."

I rub my eyes as I settle at the table. Bobby, wearing nothing but an apron, moves around the kitchen with effortless ease. When he bends to grab something from the refrigerator, I glance away quickly, surprised at his confidence. He returns with a tray holding two bowls, spoons, and a glass kettle full of milk.

"I've got Frosted Flakes, Kashi, and Lucky Charms."

"Bobby, you shouldn't have. I could have made breakfast."

"Not for my lady. Just because I'm rich doesn't mean I don't know my way around the kitchen."

"This is regular milk?" I ask.

"Oh, excuse me. Just a second." He gets up, retrieves a different container from the fridge, and sets it down with a small, apologetic smile. "Here you go. My apologies."

I steal a glance at him, admiring the way the morning light softens the edges of his unshaven jaw. There's something undeniably magnetic about him.

"So, Miss Thesia. Have you given any further thought to my proposal?"

"How long do I have to make a decision?"

"I would like to wrap up negotiations within a week so we can close the deal before the first of the month."

"It sounds so...technical when you say it like that."

"I don't mean to, but plans have to be made. The makeovers, the role players. Things have to be scheduled. I really hope you decide to do this."

"I'll think about it."

After breakfast, I find myself staring at my reflection in the bathroom mirror. What does he see in me that he can't get from just about anyone else? I'm just…okay. Not particularly striking, not overly interesting. And he certainly doesn't want me for my money. So, what gives?

I grab my phone from my purse. Ten missed calls. Eight from Tease, two from Dumas. Guilt prickles at me—I should have checked in last night. I press the call button, and Tease answers immediately.

"Where the hell are you?"

And good morning to you too, I think dryly.

"I'm with Bobby."

"Where? Here in Pittsburgh?"

"No, we're at his cabin in the woods. Up near Punxsutawney."

"He hooked up with you last night, didn't he? I can tell in your voice."

"Why would you say that?"

"Oh my god. He did! You giant whore! How was it?"

I peek out the bathroom door, making sure Bobby is nowhere nearby, then close it softly. "It was amazing."

"Oh my god, oh my god! So tell me. Was he big? I bet he was big. Average? That's okay. Tell me. I can't believe this, you total whore bag."

"Would you calm down? I don't want to talk about this right now. I've got to go. I'll be back this evening."

"So, about six inches? That's a good size. Was he eight? Ten? No way. Was he?"

"We didn't have a damn tape measure. Is that all you care about?"

"Okay, okay. Sorry. So, how was his—"

"Oh my God. You wouldn't believe it, Tease. Pure perfection." I stop mid-sentence as something unsettling dawns on me. He wants me to be his partner. But deep down, is there a part of me that wants to be... something more to him?

"Annis? Annis? You there?"

"I gotta go, Tease. See you tonight."

I hang up and step into the large shower. The marble tiles are smooth under my feet as the water warms and cascades over me, washing away the remnants of last night. Steam fills the room, fogging the glass shower door.

"Annis, are you alright?" Bobby's voice is muffled through the door.

"Um...yes, Bobby. I'm fine. I'll be out in a moment."

As I lather my hair, I notice a message forming in the condensation on the glass. Bobby is writing something—but not with his finger. I squint at the backward letters until the meaning clicks.

"That's quite a pen you have there, Mr. Beige."

He slides into the shower, grinning. "I've gotten dirty. I need someone to bathe me."

I take the soap and work up a lather, running my fingers across his back and down to his waist. The moment is playful, teasing—until I realize I'm slowly freezing because he's hogging the hot water. I nudge forward, claiming my share, and we laugh as we switch places back and forth.

"Dammit. This isn't working. Face forward."

I turn, the water now hitting my chest in a soothing cascade. He moves in close behind me, his breath warm against my neck.

"You are dirty," I murmur.

"I'm dirty everywhere, Miss Thesia," he whispers back.

Afterward, as we step out of the shower, he wraps a towel around me and smirks. "Remind me to draw up plans for a bigger shower in the Rec Room."

I roll my eyes, making a goofy face, which earns me a playful slap on my backside.

On the blimp ride back to Pittsburgh, Bobby hands me a folder filled with papers. "Read these when you have time," he says. He also presents a box of books and DVDs from his collection. A quick glance at the titles makes my stomach flip—there's no way I can let Tease get her hands on these.

As we land and he walks me to my door, he lifts my hand to his lips and kisses it softly.

"You please me, Miss Thesia."

"And you please me, Mr. Beige. I may have murmured."

His smile lingers as he steps back. "You've got a lot of homework regarding our agreement. I'll check in soon. Deal?"

I exhale deeply, feeling the weight of it all. "Deal."

Chapter 10

I walk into the apartment and hear Tease yacking on her phone in the bedroom. This gives me the chance to rush my box full of porn stuff into my room without her knowing. I slide it under the bed for later. Why do I feel like a teenage boy?

I fix my hair in the mirror, take a deep breath, and step into the living room, bracing myself for the barrage of questions I know is coming. As I pour a glass of Wild Turkey in the kitchen, I pause, reflecting on everything that has happened this weekend. Just last week, I was single and celibate. Today, I'm dating someone and sexually active. My body tingles just thinking about Bobby Beige. I'm also sore in a place I never believed could actually be sore.

Tease catches me as I walk from the kitchen to the couch.

"Oh, my God. Look at you. You walk like you just got off a cattle drive."

"I feel like I just got off a cattle drive."

"Wow. Congratulations! Welcome to whoreville, roomie."

"Thanks. I think."

"So?"

"So, what?"

"Don't make me beat you up. I want to know what it was like. It's been so long for me I can't remember what my first time was actually like. I just know it was brief. C'mon. Give it up."

"After the game, we flew from the stadium to his cabin in the woods."

"You flew? He has his own plane? Of course he does, he's rich."

"Not on a plane." I catch myself grinning, remembering the magical feeling.

"He's got a helicopter. Oh my God, that's incredible?"

"A blimp, actually."

Her eyes widen. "No way! He took you to his love cabin on a blimp? How fucking romantic is that? Go on."

"Well, it's a unique place out there. Beautiful. Peaceful. We had a great weekend."

"I don't care about that! How was the sex? Did he hurt you?"

"No. No. Of course not. He was patient, tender, and loving. He was aware of my... inexperience... so he kept it pretty normal. I guess."

"Normal? Is that what he called it? Normal?"

"Those are my words, not his. I thought it was amazing."

"How many times?"

"Tease!"

"C'mon, tell me. How many times? Give it up like you did with him."

I hold up six fingers, and her mouth drops.

"Six times or six orgasms?"

"Six times and twelve orgasms, I think."

"Holy shit, girl. He must be some sort of sick sex machine. No wonder you can hardly walk. Damn."

I did not want to answer that question. He is a sick sex machine. She doesn't know the half of it. I was his little plaything all weekend, and I liked it.

"So, since you were new, I suppose he left your ass alone."

"What do you mean?"

"Anal sex, Annis. Back door entry. Trust me, you'd know it if he did it."

"Oh, no. They really want to do that?"

"Usually not with brand-new relationships, so you should be good for a while, but eventually, you'll have to give it up."

"I'm really not comfortable with that."

"Look, I used to have a strict 'Exit Only' policy myself. But, you drink enough, you lube enough, get in the right position—it's not that bad. The guy always sticks it in there like it's a mistake, but it's never a mistake. They know exactly what they are doing. Sick horny bastards."

"You've done that? Really?"

She nods. "Look, it's not my favorite, but ever since the damn Internet, it's all they think about. They can be young, middle-aged, or old. Doesn't matter. They will eventually want to stick it in your ass. If you know this, you can at least be prepared. Make them get you off first before you let them in back there. It's harder to cum, but I've actually had an orgasm a time or two doing it."

"It seems so unnatural and kinky."

"That's the point, darling. The more they are not supposed to do it, the more they want to do it."

Luckily, all the disturbing images running through my brain are wiped clean by the doorbell ringing. Standing outside is a UPS man in brown.

"Delivery for Miss Thesia," he says, handing me a package about the size of a shoebox. I sign his tablet and bring it inside.

"It's from Beige Enterprises," I say, reading the note.

"Open it!" Tease says, sitting up on the couch.

I rip the strip tag, and inside are two antique baseballs. One is signed by Honus Wagner and the other by Roberto Clemente—two Hall of Fame members of the Pittsburgh Pirates.

Holy cow. These have to be worth a small fortune. Inside is a note.

Dear Miss Thesia,

Since you did so well taking care of mine, I wanted to send you these. I look forward to seeing you again.

BB

"What kind of guy sends a girl a couple of balls?" Tease says, getting up and heading to the kitchen. She is not a Pirates fan.

"A wonderful one, that's who. You have no clue what these are worth. This is a tremendous gift. Now, I do feel like a whore."

"Why would you feel that way? Whores fuck for money. You fucked for some collectible balls. There is no relation."

Maybe she's right. We just happened to have had some sex. He was thankful, so he sent me a gift. I look up their value on Tease's computer. The Wagner ball is worth $6,000, and the Clemente ball is going for $8,000. Tease is more impressed after I explain it all to her.

"At least you're not a cheap whore, I'll give you that."

"So, you think I should keep these?" I ask.

"Of course you're not going to keep them. You're going to auction them first thing in the morning and get that cash! Then go get yourself something cool."

She doesn't understand. I take Bobby's balls back to my bedroom and close the door. I set them side-by-side on my nightstand and reach underneath my bed to pull out some of the materials he gave me for my homework. The first book is on sexual role-playing, an encyclopedia of scenarios organized by century and decade.

I flip through the pages, looking at various photographs. The images make me feel warm, so I take off my shirt and pants, sitting on the bed in just my bra and panties.

There are full backstories provided for the following scenarios:
- Ben Franklin/Martha Washington
- Plantation Owner/Slave Girl
- Abe Lincoln/John Wilkes Booth (I don't think so.)
- Policeman/Tramp
- George Custer/Indian Squaw
- Fireman/School Teacher

I find a small post-it note beside the next one:

Billionaire/Simpleton

So, he thinks of me as a simpleton? I make a mental note to find out what that means.

Looking at this book makes me think of him. I reach over and grab both his balls. I smile, remembering our time together this weekend. I rub them against my face, enjoying their smoothness—until I realize, with horror, that I've been licking them.

Oh shit. The autographs!

Shit. Shit. Shit.

Chapter 11

This is my last week at Lowe's. I'd like to say I'm going to miss this place, but hey, it's Lowe's. Near the end of my shift at the register, a very fit man in a suit approaches me.

"Miss Thesia?"

"Yes?"

"Mr. Beige would like to see you as soon as your shift is complete. He's awaiting you outside in the car."

"Okay. Thanks."

That's odd. He wasn't supposed to meet me until Wednesday. That means he wants to see me just as much as I want to see him. I haven't completed all my homework on the materials he gave me, but I know a lot more now than I did before all this started. He wants to be dominated, mothered, pampered, served, and disciplined. That's what I've gathered. What I don't know is if I'm up for it. I've never been a boss of anything or anyone. Why couldn't we just make out like we did that first weekend at the love cabin? I'll see what he says.

The muscle man in the suit opens the door for me in the parking lot, and I slide into the backseat of a brand-new Tesla. The windows are heavily tinted, and the interior smells like Bobby. The scent hits my senses and goes straight to my loins. Shit. I didn't wear a pad today. He wasn't supposed to be here.

"Your driver?" I ask.

"And other things. His name is Lurch. How are you, Miss Thesia? I can't express how deeply I have missed you."

"It's only been two days, Bobby."

"Two of the longest days of my life. I literally... ache for you."

"I missed you too."

"That's good to know. I was worried since you didn't text

me."

"My phone doesn't have a keyboard. It's a pain to text, so I just don't do it."

"I was afraid of that," he says, reaching into his breast pocket and taking out an iPhone. "I hope you like pink. I know I do. You don't even have to type your texts. Just speak into the phone and hit send. It's amazingly easy."

Tease loves her iPhone. It feels nice in my hand, and I do like the pink cover he put on it. I turn it on, and it makes a nice little bird tweet sound.

"That means you have a text," he says.

I slide my finger across the screen to unlock the device and tap the message.

Dear Annis, It's Bobby. I want to fuck.

I smile. Oh, how sweet. Next message.

Dear Annis, Lowe's sucks. It's hot out here in the parking lot.

I giggle. Next message.

Annis, seriously. It's too hot. Get your ass out here.

"I was getting a little impatient."

"Thanks, Bobby, but you shouldn't have done this."

But I've always wanted one! He gave me an iPhone! He gave me an iPhone! He's my boyfriend! My rich boyfriend!

"I need to be able to reach you at any time, Annis. It was nothing. We set the account up at Beige Enterprises."

"You can't just keep giving me all this stuff. Do you know how much those baseballs are worth?"

"Not really. I got them out of some case at the stadium. Hundred bucks, maybe?"

"No, more like about fourteen thousand dollars."

"WHAT?" He grabs his chest.

"They are signed by Hall of Fame players. They are easily worth that."

"I had no idea. Dammit!" His breathing gets stressed.

"Don't worry. You can have them back."

"Really? That would be great. I'll get you something more reasonable. Fourteen thousand? Fuck me. I'll send Lurch over to pick them up. I really had no idea. I just thought sending you a couple of balls was romantic." His breathing starts to slow down.

"I understand. It's not a problem."

I don't have the heart to tell him I kind of ruined them with my licking. Serves him right for being such a cheap bastard. Why on earth are we in a Tesla?

Regaining his breath, he turns to me and models that cute face, those cute eyes, and those cute, luscious lips.

"Have you thought about our proposal? I'm very hopeful the merger can be completed."

"I'm just unsure that I can be all you want me to be in this relationship, Bobby. It's a bit weird."

"Oh, but Annis. The places I can take you. The time I can take you to. The places and time I can take you. And all the fucking."

He gently reaches over and starts stroking my hand. Oh, his touch. Wow.

"Yes, I know. Bizarrely. I've done some reading, but I'm not ready to commit."

"Will you at least consent to a colonic treatment before this weekend? I'll go with you and hold your hand. It will be romantic."

"I've been reading about those as well. Some people say those treatments don't do any more for you than your body does on its own."

He lets my hand go and pulls back to the far side of the back seat.

"Well. Those people… are just wrong! They are wrong, hear me? They are full of shit, and that's their problem! It has changed my life. Don't listen to them, Annis. Trust me on this. I'll be with you. You will feel so much better. I'm concerned about your health."

I cross my eyes. "Whatever."

"Please, don't do that."

"What? This?" I cross them and move toward him.

"Annis, please. Look what you're doing to me."

Bobby Beige has a bulge. I take my left hand and grab it hard. He yelps just a little.

"Listen to me, Bobby. I'll sign your agreement when I'm good and ready, understand?" I tighten my grip. His eyes open wide in shock.

"Yes…Ma'am."

"Now, I want you to take me in this car. This fucking little electric car." I let go of my grip and start unbuttoning my jeans. I try to take them off but I forgot to take off my shoes. "Shit."

Bobby is undoing his belt and pants and can't believe I just talked to him like that. I was dominant. I reach down and try to undo my shoelaces. Why is this so difficult? I'm bent over so long the blood rushes to my head giving me a headache. Bobby tries to keep the momentum going by touching my breasts as I'm bent over. I get one shoe off. That will have to do. I look over at him and his pants are open and ready for business. I remember how small he is until he's fully aroused, so I reach in and try to fish the thing out. I find it and he whimpers just a bit as I start stroking it. I slip off my panties as best I can. My pants and underwear end up all bundled around my left leg because of that damn stubborn shoe.

"Oh, Annis," he moans.

"Shuttup!" I shout and then I slap him across the face with my right hand. Not too hard, just a slap.

That did it. He basically explodes out of his pants and I stare at his giant obelisk with a pink dome. I throw my free leg over his groin and try to mount my dripping lady parts on top of him, but the ceiling of the Tesla is too low. Dammit. I bend my neck so I can get a bit higher. All I need is a few more inches and I can mount him. I now have my shoulders pressing up against the roof of the tiny car. Bobby lowers his ass forward in the seat to make more room but it doesn't work. He's too big. I can't get on it. His knees are rubbing against the seats in front of us. He can't get any lower. I try rubbing my self on his shaft but that only makes the torture worse. We're so close.

My chin comes to rest on the top of his head. I'm distracted by the sweet smell of his hair. It's lovely. Then I go back to work. I've got to get that thing inside me and get it inside me now!

Bobby is groaning and manages to get his hands underneath my shirt before getting them caught on the underwire of by bra. The underwire is so tight, he can't reach my nipples with his fingertips so he gently massages my underboob as if that's going to turn me on.

We wrestle in the tiny back seat of that stupid car for ten more minutes. We are sweating and the windows quickly fog over. I start to get lightheaded and slow down. We've lost it. The momentum is gone and I gently slide off him and back to my side of the back seat. Bobby shrinks quicker than a balloon and disappears deep inside his britches. We take a moment to catch our breath.

"Well...shit," I say.

"My sentiments exactly."

"Get a bigger car for God's sake. Don't drive a pussy car. You're a man. You want to have sex in a car, get a decent...fucking...car!"

"Yes...Ma'am."

"Thesia out!"

And I leave.

Chapter 12

By the time I got home, my new pink phone was chirping with text messages. I ignored them. I was driving, and he should know better than to expect me to text behind the wheel. Then again, he has a driver—what does he care?

I tossed my bag onto the bed and sprawled out before finally checking my phone.

Text Message from BobbyB: That was so hot. You slapped me. I had no idea you could be such a bitch.

Text Message from BobbyB: Sorry I called you a bitch. You may have to discipline me.

Text Message from BobbyB: I got you this phone so you would be in communication with me. I don't like to wait. Please don't be a bitch about this.

Text Message from BobbyB: Answer me, Bitch!

Text Message from BobbyB: I'm sorry I called you bitch again. I'm worried. Please call. I'm the only number saved in your phone. All you have to do is click one button and say, "Call Bobby." I don't want you using it to speak to anyone else but me.

Text Message from BobbyB: I don't get it. I get you this device and you don't use it. Are you being mean, or are you just too stupid?

Text Message from BobbyB: I'm sorry I called you stupid. You're not stupid. But making me mad like this is not very smart. You do know I'm rich, right?

Text Message from BobbyB: I haven't used the FRR in weeks. I want you to join me there. I want you to enjoy the pleasures of the FRR with me. I'm going to self-pleasure here in the car if you don't contact me.

Text Message from BobbyB: I can't text now. I'm

self-pleasuring. @np78iqwnl;'hg

Text Message from BobbyB: I'm relaxed and sipping some wine in the back of the Tesla. I was just involved in a car-jacking! LOL.

Text Message from BobbyB: I hate my life. I'm rich, successful, but I really have no friends. Except for you, and you won't text me back. WTF?

Text Message from BobbyB: I just took a Percocet and half a Demerol. Call me, text me, or not. I don't really give a shit.

Wow. I had no idea he was this needy. I tapped out a reply.

Text Message to BobbyB: I was driving. If you are truly concerned with my health, you won't require me to text while driving. You seriously need to chill out.

My phone immediately chirped again.

Text Message from BobbyB: Hey baby. Noooo, man, I'm cool. I'm going to take a nap, I think. You insulted my car, man. Not cool. I just got this thing. It gets like... a bajillion miles a gallon. You left me here. I had to suck my own dick. Not cool. Do you know how hard that is to do? I think Lurch saw me doing it. Get your colon cleared out.

He was stoned out of his mind. I wondered if he could actually do that to himself. My mind tried to picture it, and all I could imagine was him bending over like a dog. He was young, flexible, and long. Maybe he was telling the truth. Doubtful.

Lurch knocked on my door. I handed him the two baseballs. He made a weird face, then passed me a bouquet of flowers, a box of chocolates, and a Pirates cap. Some trade that was. He'd pay for that move.

I had until tomorrow night to wrap my head around this whole Dominant/Submissive thing Bobby was into. The videos

I watched were uncomfortable and embarrassing. I had to keep adjusting the volume so Tease wouldn't hear. Most featured men punishing women, which I couldn't stomach. But the ones where women were in control... those were interesting. Some even turned me on a little.

I found illustrations showing the best spots for spanking, charts detailing which areas produced pleasure versus pain. The section on prostate stimulation made me wince, but the pleasure it gave the guys made me consider it. This was about Bobby and me—giving and receiving pleasure. Who was I to judge what was normal? Maybe this messed-up world of his was just reality for him. But for me? A huge adjustment.

The adult breastfeeding video disturbed me—grown men feeding from grown women, some wearing diapers. And not weirdos, either. Attractive, successful people. Some even did it in public—on subways, in parks.

Bobby had included a 200-page, full-color catalog of Submissive & Dominant gear in my box. So many outfits, sex toys, whips, chains, paddles. And, of course, all available with free two-day shipping. How convenient.

Then there was the inter-species stuff. I shoved those DVDs, magazines, and books to the bottom of the box without looking. I didn't even want to think about it. Though I was tempted to watch the one titled Why Democrats Really Love Donkeys. Looked funny. Still gross.

Everything I read emphasized the ass. Maybe Tease was right—maybe Bobby really wanted to go there. But I wasn't ready. I had just figured out how my pussy worked. Why would I move two inches down? It had another purpose—one I didn't find glamorous.

Apparently, there were Ass Games held every four years at an exclusive adult resort. People picked up objects with their butts, played relay races, even blew up balloons. Tease would excel at that last one. She could clear a room like a champ.

I needed to clear my mind. I grabbed Tease and we called Dumas. Time for drinks.

At our favorite bar a couple blocks away, Tease zeroed in on the cutest guy in the room. Within an hour, they were making out on the pool table.

Two beers in, and I was already buzzed. Dumas handed me a Long Island Iced Tea, and that was it. I was wasted. Loud music meant we had to yell even though we were two feet apart.

"Dumas? Dumbass. Whatever your name is!"

"Yes, Annis?"

"You're gay. Why don't you just admit it?"

"No. You're wrong. I'm not! I just have a sense for fashion and a somewhat feminine voice. But trust me. I'm not gay!"

"What is it with men's obsession with anal sex?"

Silence. The music had stopped. Everyone in the bar had heard me. Dumas stared in horror. A few guys down the bar leaned in, grinning.

"Oh, like none of you have ever asked that question!"

The music kicked back in, the bar noise resumed.

"I'm going to call Bobby," I announced, reaching for my phone.

"No, I don't think that's a good idea," Dumas said, trying to stop me. Too late.

"Beige."

"You sick bastard. Why do you want things in your ass? Why? Why do you want to put stuff in my ass?"

"Annis?"

"Get away, Dumas. I'm talking to him. Stop it! It's my phone."

"Annis, are you okay? Where are you?"

"Is that why you want me to get a colon cleansing? Huh? Is that why?"

"Annis, tell me where you are."

"Maybe I don't want a colon cleansing! Maybe my colon is

fine for what it's meant to do! Theesia out! Bitch."

My phone started ringing. I ignored it, laughing at what I'd just said. Dumas wasn't laughing. Especially when Bobby and Lurch appeared behind me.

"Annis?"

I turned. "Oh, if it isn't the ass man and his bouncer. How'd you get here so fast?"

"You're drunk. Let me take you home," Bobby says.

"I don't think so. I'm not that easy. Woo me."

Bobby sighed, pulled out a hundred-dollar bill. "Here."

"You're cheap."

Bobby threw me over his shoulder. The last thing I remembered was my head bouncing against the Tesla's doorway.

Chapter 13

I wake up in the bedroom of Bobby's love cabin, immediately recognizing the scent of the logs. I'm naked beneath the covers. Music drifts in from the great room. The hardwood floor is cold against my feet as I stand. On the dresser, Bobby has laid out fresh clothes. The panties are sheer, black, and barely-there. Next to them, a bottle of water and a container of Advil. He's so thoughtful.

As I slip the panties on, something catches my attention—I'm shaved. Holy crap! Did I do that last night?

There's also a strange tingling sensation in my rear that I can't explain. Would he have done something while I was unconscious? No. That would be like—no, I don't even want to think about it. He's got some explaining to do.

"Ah, there you are," he says as I half-stumble into the kitchen. "How are you feeling?"

"Like I got hit by a bus." He hands me a large cup of coffee, and I settle onto a counter stool. "You mind explaining what happened last night?"

"Starting when?"

"I don't know. Last thing I remember was being mad at you at a bar. Start from there."

"Yes, well. You were very rude. And very drunk. Lurch and I brought you out here. Since you were already here and relaxed, I made some other calls."

"What kind of other calls?"

"First, I called my Asian spa associates. Do you feel differently?"

"I knew it! You had them wax me, didn't you? How could I not feel that?"

"Oh no, my dear Annis. The Asian girls were for me. I had them give me a massage. I shaved you myself. First, I had to use a heavy-duty hair trimmer to prep the area, then I got down to the skin after a couple of passes with razors. I ruined a few in the process..."

"Okay, I get it."

"But after a while, I think I got you in nice shape. Not as good as a wax, but smooth."

That's... weird. He shaved me himself. I don't feel any cuts or nicks, which means he must have experience. Of course, he does.

"So, why does my ass feel weird? You didn't do what I think you might have done, did you?"

"And what would that be, Annis? Have unconscious anal sex with you? You think I'm that bizarre?"

I cross my arms, narrowing my eyes. He smiles.

"Sex is a two-to-five-person act, Miss Thesia. You need feedback. Who would play an instrument if it didn't produce any sound? Only the deaf. And I am not deaf."

"So, again, I ask—why does my ass feel weird?"

"That, my dear, is the sweet sensation of total cleanliness and health."

My mouth drops. "You didn't."

"Oh, we did. Trust me. You really needed it. I'll spare you the details..."

"We?"

"The Asian girls are licensed in hydrotherapy as well. They're very good. You slept through the entire thing. I was so proud of you."

While I'm shocked, I have to admit—I do feel different. And, oddly, in a good way. But the idea of strangers administering such an embarrassing and personal treatment is disturbing. My head throbs. I down four Advil, but I doubt they'll be enough.

"So, is a massage all the Asian girls did for you last night?"

He smiles. "Oh, hell no. Those girls are very talented. I wish you could have been there to see it, to partake in it with me. There was a virtual tornado of pleasure that took place in the FRR last night."

"Is that how this relationship is going to be, Bobby?" I snap. "Every time I can't be your sex toy because of my irresponsible behavior, you go out and get some Asian prostitutes?"

"For your information, they are whores, not prostitutes."

"What's the difference?"

"Trust me. There's a big difference. You'll find out what I mean tonight. I've invited them back for this evening."

"You what? I don't want to meet your whores! I'm your whore!"

That didn't come out right. Bobby raises an eyebrow as he sips his coffee.

"Don't give me that look," I say, raising my hand and looking away. "You know what I meant. I'm not with other guys, Bobby. You shouldn't be with other women. That's common courtesy in any relationship."

"You should know by now, Annis, that I am anything but common. Neither of us has signed off on our agreement. You are not with other guys because no other guys are currently after you the way I am. For you, it's much less of a sacrifice. But never mind all that. I want to finish these negotiations today so we can begin your training."

"My training?"

"Yes. You can't expect to just go into the FRR and know what to do. It takes time. You just had sex for the first time the other night. What you are about to embark on is way beyond that. You have to discover your inner slut."

How does he know about her?

As much as I hate to admit it, he's right. I need to open up a bit and welcome new things. If this is what it takes to be with him, then so be it. How many women have done things they didn't want to for a man? But he's not just any man. He's billionaire Bobby Beige. Beautiful, billionaire Bobby Beige. I bet he's French kissing the rim of that coffee mug right now. He's so hot. I want him between my legs.

Oh, shit. I didn't bring pads for my panties. Of course, you didn't, idiot—you were abducted at a bar for being an asshole.

"Alright. What do we need to do to get started?" I ask.

"Well, you've seen my hard limits. We need to come up with yours."

Bobby gestures for me to sit at the dining room table. He grabs his laptop, opens a copy of the AGREEMENT, and scrolls down before sliding me closer so I can see the screen. He smells so good.

"Would you like to put limits on what can be inserted into your anal cavity?"

"Yeah, how about nothing!"

"Annis, my dear. How can you judge something for which you have no knowledge?"

"I'm sorry, Bobby, but I don't think I need to be experienced to make a judgment call on that one."

"That is where you are wrong, Miss Thesia. Let me help you out. Let's start with limits on smaller-diameter sex toys, vibrators, and the like. Only about the width of... a magic marker. See? Look at mine. It's small. You'll hardly know it's there. We'll see how you handle those, then readdress the issue once you have some knowledge of how to really think about it."

Maybe he's right. Until I really know.

I consent.

Hard Limits (For Dominant)

The following items shall only be allowed in the anal cavity of the Dominant:

1. Small-diameter items.

I position myself in front of the keyboard and copy some of his hard limits—like the bowels, bladder, and vomiting stuff. Gross. Also, I do not want my heart stopped. Then, as my own limits, I type:

- The Dominant will NOT perform, watch, or be involved in any sexual activity regarding animals of any kind.
- The Dominant will not be subject to any mocking of skin problems, foot odor, nose hair, back arm fat, kankles, vaginal smells, shoes, or anything related to general appearance.

"What are kankles?" he asks.

"Oversized ankles. Like… Hillary Clinton."

Bobby nods in agreement. "Okay, I see where you're going. But when it comes to animals, how about stuffed animals?"

"Oh, whatever, I'm just not doing anything with that goat or donkey you have down there. Hear me?"

"Okay, okay. But he will be disappointed. He's very gentle and loving."

Even though he's smiling like it's a joke, I can't be 100% sure he actually is joking. I have a strong feeling this guy has done some things down there that are not right in any way, shape, or form.

"Is there anything down here where I could get hurt?" I ask.

"Most of the pain comes from the Dominant to the Submissive. So, no, not really. However, you could slip and fall. You could pass out from exhaustion. There have been times of organ displacement inside the female lower torso due to my—"

"Yeah, I get that."

"I will not harm you in any way during our pleasuring of one another. But, I do tend to suck really hard, so you may feel some discomfort in your breasts."

He likes to suck…hard. That's kind of hot. We go through the entire list and I feel okay about what I'm about to sign. This is scary and exhilarating at the same time.

"The last matter of business is our safe word," he says.

"Safe word?"

"Yes, that's what you say when you want anything that is going on down there to stop immediately."

"Oh, okay. Well, let me think. I've got it. Mind will be... STOP!"

"Alright, Stop," he says as he taps the keypad. "I've got that keyed into the contract. Should be easy to remember."

"My safe word is midget."

"Why midget?"

"I'd rather not discuss it. But whenever you hear me say it, you stop whatever it is that you are doing to me."

"I understand," I say with a slight giggle. "Have you ever had to actually say it?"

"What, the safe word?" I nod. "One time. Many years ago when I was much younger."

"Would you consider this...relationship a success if I actually made you say it during one of our sessions in the FRR?"

"You are a novice, Annis. If you abide by my hard limits, I can see no scenario where you would actually get me to say it. So, the answer is yes. You accomplish that, and you will have surprised me beyond my wildest dreams."

"MIDGET!!" I say with a smile.

"Okay, now you're mocking me. Do I have to put in the contract that you are restricted from mocking the safe word?"

"No, but if I did make fun, all you have to do is say, MIDGET!"

Chapter 14

I spend the day exploring Bobby's property. Later, we take a walk around all the land he owns. It's beautiful out here—well-maintained grounds, clear trails, a small lake, winding creeks, and a bluff overlooking the mountains. Bobby is a fast hiker, and I struggle to keep up.

"You'll have to get into better shape, Annis. You must take care of your body. I've arranged for your personal trainer to begin working with you next week."

"I...GASP...don't need....HUFF WHEEZE....a fff....GASP....a damn....HUFF WHEEZE HUFF...trainer."

I bend over, placing both palms on my knees, trying to catch my breath. Bobby, standing nearby, checks his heartbeat with some sort of gadget.

"Just listen to you. We've come less than half a mile."

HUFF WHEEZE HUFF WHEEZE HUFF WHEEZE.

"This is not even an incline. We've been walking downhill the entire way. The FRR is no place for wimps, Miss Thesia. You will get in shape, or this is not going to work."

I nod in understanding, still unable to speak more than a word or two. Eventually, he carries me back to the cabin like a football player training with tires strapped to his back. Even after jogging with me weighing him down, he barely breaks a sweat when we get inside. Oh, but I can smell it—divine. I'd like to lick it off his forehead or his neck. Maybe not the balls just yet. But maybe.

After showering, a chef prepares us a wonderful meal. We have delicious wine, and as soft music plays, Bobby takes my hands and leads me in a romantic dance on the patio beneath a bright moon. It's magical. He's gorgeous. I've never felt this way about anyone before. My legs ache from the hike, but I keep slow dancing to the soft, romantic sounds of Satisfaction by The Rolling Stones.

I want to cross my eyes at him, but I know how it affects his libido. He's looking at me. Why doesn't he say something? I want to, but I don't know what. Maybe he'll start, and then I can just respond. He looks like he wants to say something.

Come on, Bobby. Say it. Tell me how you feel.

He looks at his watch.

"Time to fuck."

Not exactly what I was hoping for, but it communicates a certain level of affection. He cares for me. Am I the one for him? He could be with anyone, but he has chosen me… and perhaps some Asian hookers. I'm so lucky. Life is good.

Still, I feel apprehensive about what's to come. We step into the elevator, and he stops to look at me.

"Are you ready for this?"

I take a deep breath, squeeze his hand, and nod. He smiles. As we exit the elevator, the scene explodes with life. Where did all these people come from? Someone just rode a horse down the street. A real horse. It looks like tonight is western night.

City noises surround me—gunshots in the background, people shouting, dogs barking. Lights flash and move. Neon signs buzz, Open.

"You need to go in here first," Bobby says, leading me to an OBGYN office. "Dr. Probass will take care of you. When you're done, step into the costume shop and then come over to the saloon in the hotel. I'll be waiting."

I open the door gently. Dr. Probass sits behind a desk, reading what looks like medical records.

"Ahhhh, Miss Thesia. I've been expecting you. Come, sit down."

He finishes reading a page and sets it aside. He's an odd-looking man in his fifties with thick glasses. Not handsome, not ugly—just odd. His hands are a bit hairy. I immediately don't like him.

"I've been asked to give you a thorough examination as preparation for tonight's festivities and others to soon follow."

"Okay."

"Do you have any of the following? Please respond yes or no. Gonorrhea?"

"No."

"Viral Hepatitis?"

"No."

"HIV or AIDS?"

"No."

"Syphilis?"

"Nope."

"Yes or no only, please. Chlamydia?"

"Who?"

"It's not a who, Miss Thesia. Chlamydia. Also known as crabs."

"Oh. No."

"Bacterial Vaginosis?"

"Um...no."

"You hesitated. Do you have BV?"

"No. I don't."

"Can you tell me what it even is?"

"It's... bacteria... on the vaginal... space area." You asshole.

He nods, rolling his eyes. "Mr. Beige didn't mention you went to medical school. What a surprise. Strip down and get up on the chair. Let's go."

"Please."

"I'm not here to be polite, Miss Thesia, or whatever the hell your name is. I don't really give a shit. I'm here to make sure Mr. Beige has a clean specimen for his activities. Now, either drop your panties and climb up on this chair, or we can all go home. Either way, I get paid. What's it going to be?"

I make a face, then turn around and do as he says. The padding on the birthing chair is cold against my skin. Instinctively, I spread my legs and place my feet in the stirrups. How humiliating is this? A small sheet barrier is raised so I don't see what he's doing. I stare at the ceiling.

Dr. Probass slides on gloves, goggles, and a mask, inspecting me like a mechanic checking an engine. What's with the goggles?

"I see you've recently been waxed or shaved. First time, wasn't it?"

"Yes."

"I can tell by the pink rash and the bumps."

He puts his nose down there and takes a big whiff. WTF?

"At least you don't smell bad. And your size appears to be average to small, which Beige will find pleasing. I've seen ones so big you could park a car inside. They didn't last a week."

I close my eyes as he continues his exam. I hate this. I absolutely hate this.

"You must be very special," he says.

"Why do you say that?"

"Beige's other women are different. He must see something in you."

"How are they different?"

"I don't know. Prettier, I suppose. More fit. Better figures. You don't seem to match those qualities, so you must be special in other ways. Good for you."

Sorry I asked.

A moment later, I hear the unmistakable click of a camera shutter. My eyes snap open. He pretends nothing happened.

"Did you just take a picture of me?"

"No."

"I could have sworn I heard an iPhone camera go off."

"Are you a doctor, Miss Thesia?"

"No."

"Then shut the fuck up and lie still."

He reaches over onto a small table and grabs a pair of tongs. Oh, shit. Just get this over with. Just get this over with. In they go and I am stretched and pulled in every direction possible. It feels like he's going to yank my labia up over my head. I lay back and close my eyes again. Another iPhone shutter click goes off.

"What the hell? I know that was a camera noise."

"No, it was this device." He holds up the tongs. "They make a strange noise."

"No it wasn't."

"Look, I'll stand up. No phone camera." He stands up, empties his pockets and turns around. Maybe I was just hearing things.

"I'm going to give you an injection. It will prevent your body from producing any eggs while you're with Mr. Beige. You won't need to worry about birth control after this; it takes care of that. For the first week, you'll need to take lactation pills once a day, and after that, you can reduce it to every few days. Mr. Beige prefers a lot of milk, so I recommend following these instructions."

"What's in the injection?" I ask, trying to sound casual.

Dr. Probass pulls out a large syringe with a small device inside. "This is the latest model. It tracks some health data, prevents pregnancy, and also has a GPS tracking feature in case you get lost or anything."

Before I can react, the needle sinks into the fat of my arm. The pain is sharp and immediate. GPS? What the hell? I can already feel my anger building—Bobby and I are going to have a serious conversation about this. After what feels like an eternity, Dr. Probass removes the needle and wipes away the small amount of blood that's trickling from the spot. He applies a Band-Aid and then rolls his chair back to his desk to make some notes on a clipboard.

Just then, a phone begins to ring. I feel a slight vibration between my legs. That sick bastard.

"Aren't you going to answer that?" I ask, my voice edged with frustration.

"Answer what?" he responds, still focused on his chart. The ringing continues, but he ignores it.

"The damn iPhone you shoved in my—"

He cuts me off, rolling his chair back between my legs. The numbness from the injection is making everything feel distant, but I'm vaguely aware as he removes the phone.

"It's fine," he murmurs into the phone, "She's fine... We're almost done. Five more minutes." He hangs up, wiping the phone with a rag as if it were nothing.

"We're done here," he says, finally. "You can get dressed. The lactation pills are on that table. Take them with food."

Chapter 15

There is a lady in the costume shop waiting for me after I left Dr. Creepy. She calls me by name, and then starts touching my different parts taking measurements. Have enough strangers touched me today?

"Oh my," she says under her breath.

I understand. I know that Bobby's other girls are thinner and prettier, and I'm getting a bit tired of hearing it from the staff. She walks to the back and, after a moment, returns with an armful of fluffy clothes. It looks like an old Western saloon girl outfit. She helps me put on the mesh stockings and then the tight-fitting bodice, pulling the strings in the back. She grunts as she tightens it, lifting my bosom upward. I try on several hats and finally decide on one with a large turquoise feather. My neck is adorned with a strand of pearls, and I wonder if they are real.

When I'm fully dressed, she sits me down in front of a mirror and begins applying the makeup. My inner slut is being summoned for the evening. She goes with some heavy blush, bright red lipstick and heavy dark eyeliner. I am the saloon whore. Time to get busy.

The shoes are awkward to walk in, but I manage to cross the street and enter the saloon. It's crowded, with men playing cards, a full bar of patrons, and a piano player performing in the corner. The air is thick with smoke and the smell of alcohol. Some of the men whistle at me, while others shout obscenities and propositions. I spot two Asian women, dressed similarly to me, working as waitresses. I don't have to guess who they are. A dwarf in a tiny cowboy outfit walks across the floor, glancing up at me and growling. It seems Mr. Beige has hired the entire cast for tonight's entertainment.

At the far end of the bar sits my man. Bobby is dressed entirely in black: a black shirt, a black hat, and black leather chaps. Beneath the chaps, he is wearing studded speedo underwear, and as he slowly turns, I catch a glimpse of a thong stretching between his lovely butt cheeks. A gold star adorns his vest—he must be the Marshall. Oh, my beating heart! His gun belt holds a dozen different beige magic markers in the tiny loops where bullets would normally go.

I walk across the saloon. He takes a drink from a frosted mug and tips his cap.

"Howdy, Ma'am."

"Howdy to you, Marshall."

"I must say you're looking mighty fine this evening."

"I'm a clean specimen, one might say."

"How was your visit with the doctor in town?"

"He's a messed up sack of shit and if I ever lay eyes on him again, I'll snip your balls off and never come back."

He takes a long drink from the mug. "I will take that under advisement. Can I buy you a drink?"

"You're going to have to buy me a lot more than a drink after what that creep did to me."

"I see my lady is displeased with me. Beer for the Lady!"

"Aren't you a bit cold in that outfit, Marshall?"

"I'm dressed appropriately for the venue, I think. I don't hear you complaining about it like you do everything else."

I reach around a slap his bare ass cheek. He puckers his lips. "Watch that mouth, Marshall. This is my saloon and you'll do as I say."

The music plays on, and I decide to get up on the bar and do a little dance. I'm not much of a dancer, but I grab the ruffles on my dress and hold them up, revealing my mesh stockings to Bobby. He grins and licks his lips. There are noises from the other patrons at the bar as well, many reaching for my legs while I tease them. This is so exhilarating! All eyes in the bar are on me as I dance, lifting my dress from side to side to the rhythm of the piano. Suddenly, a dwarf sticks his tongue out at me and shakes his head vigorously. Eww. Everything is going great until one of my heels slips on some spilled beer, and I tumble off the bar, landing hard on the floor in front of everyone.

Time seems to stand still for a moment. The noise, the music—everything fades. I notice the bar patrons looking at Bobby, who gestures with his right hand in a circular motion to encourage them to carry on. Eventually, they return to their role-play, acting as if I'm not sprawled out on the bar floor with my shoes in the air.

"Whoa there, Ma'am," Bobby says reaching a hand down to help me up. "Didn't figure you to be a tumbleweed."

"Why, I do say, sir. Can you help a desperate woman in need?"

"I certainly may. What…needs…might this woman have?"

"Perhaps there is a more private location we can discuss my…needs?"

He places my hand around his right arm and escorts me to the stairs. He is staring into my eyes as we walk. I just want to melt. When he opens the first door, I hear a loud squeal of a pig and smoke comes pouring out. Bobby slams it shut.

"Wrong door. Nothing to see here," he says as we move two doors down the hallway. This is more like it. A large king-sized bed with oversized pillows. There is fake moonlight shining through the window and a few candles are burning on an antique dresser drawer. The music has changed to Sexy and I Know It by LMFAO. It's some sort of extended dance mix that goes on forever. The beat gets me going. I look over at Bobby who already has his vest and shirt off. His skin is glimmering in the candlelight. This is so sexy. My love juices immediately start making their way down south.

"I've got passion in my pants, Miss Thesia. I ain't afraid to show it," he whispers as he takes a deep inhale of one of his markers.

"Marshall. I may have broken the law!"

"You need to be interrogated. Over and over."

"Interrogate me, Marshall. Hard!"

I snap open the clamps to his chaps and they fall to the ground. I'm less than a foot away from his black speedo. He shakes his tiny looking wiener around like a helicopter as the lyrics say, "Wiggle, wiggle, wiggle, wiggle, wiggle, yeah."

Although it doesn't look like much shaking in that speedo, I know the beast that is within. He pushes me back on the bed and lifts my legs in the air. He grabs my shoe heels with his teeth and pulls them off my feet. Next, he tears my black mesh stockings away and throws them against the wall. He does all this in perfect timing to the erotic beat of LMFAO. He looks amazing with his black cowboy hat still on. Take me, Cowboy!

While massaging my calf, he starts sucking on my toes one by one. Oh my! This is new.

"Ah, there is your little Japanese tattoo. Remember what it means?"

"Yes," I groan. I need to get that thing removed. I want to scream when he puts half my foot into his wet mouth. He moves his talented tongue in between each toe and then repeats the procedure moving from foot to foot. He groans a little. I groan a lot, and loud. I take a quick glance at his speedo. The beast has awakened. That small bit a fabric won't hold him much longer. I close my eyes and take in the sensation. Toes, go figure. Wow!

The door to the room opens and I'm shocked to see the two Asian waitresses come into the room. Bobby stops his toe work and says, "Ah, thanks for coming ladies. Annis, I'd like to introduce you to Makme and Miow. They will be assisting us this evening. Ladies, this is Annis."

What? Just how are they going to assist us?

Before I can even finish that thought, Bobby has handed over my elevated feet to the two girls. They take over where he left off and Oh, My, God! They go to work. I close my eyes and try to forget they are women. All ten of my toes are enjoying the pleasures of trained Asian masseuses. While they suck, they gently massage my legs moving ever slowly downward into my thighs. They are getting a bit close to my pink canoe, but for some reason I don't say anything. This is amazing. I open my eyes and Bobby is looking down at me. He has moved opposite the girls and is hovering over me from the other side of the bed.

"I told you they were good."

I cross my eyes. He immediately starts kissing me. It's weird because our faces are backward, like in that Spiderman movie. But, it is soooo hot. I've got tongues on both my feet and one deep in my mouth. I think I'm murmuring. Bobby reaches down and fondles my breasts. He tries to reach skin, but the bodice is too tight. I try to say something, but all he does is place his index finger on my lips and say, "Shhhhhh."

The Asian girls somehow manage to remove my panties and they take turns sliding fingers in and out of me. My liquid essence is flowing. Bobby is massaging my face, kissing my nose, licking my forehead. "Be very still," he says.

Taking both his thumbs, he opens my right eyelid wide, and then he licks my eyeball.

"Aaaacck!" I say.

"Shhhhh. Relax, Annis." He does it again. This time deeper and longer.

"Aaaack!"

"Shhhhh. Feel my tongue fuck your eyeball." He moves to the other eye and repeats the process.

"Aaa...ck," is all I can say. My body is getting over-stimulated. I've got too many things touching, probing and licking that I can't concentrate on any of them. The Asian girls have gone full throttle masturbation on my lower end. Am I gay now? Bobby continues his oral assault on my eyeballs. My vision is getting blurry. I've got nothing to do with my hands, so I reach up behind my head and find Bobby's speedo with a familiar item sticking out of it. I start massaging it. He groans.

The opti-sex halts for a moment while Bobby reaches over and coats his fingers with some KY lubricant. Oh, shit. What's next? The Asian girls are now kissing one another and taking off their clothes. This is some sort of wacked out dream. Bobby squirts some of the lubricant on my hands. I resume stroking him.

"That's it, Miss Thesia. The Marshall will find your daughter. You have nothing to worry about. Ohhhhh. Yeeessss. That's it. Yessss."

He feels good. I'm ashamed to think about it, but the Asian girls feel really good. I feel good. This is the most mind blowing thing I have ever experienced.

Bobby reaches down beside my head and puts both his lubricated index fingers into my ears. He slides them all around and then deep into my ear canals. Back and forth he goes with his fingers. Oh, my God. He's fucking my ears. It feels like he's touching my brain on both sides of my head. His fingers are so big and thick.

Things get intense after that. My pelvis is thrusting up to the rhythm of the music to get more action from the Asian girls. They are now totally naked and kissing one another as they massage me downstairs. I'm stroking Bobby's massive schlong above my head and he his thrusting his hips forward and moaning. All this is happening while his index fingers are going in and out of my ears and his tongue is stimulating my eyeballs. We all cum within seconds of each other. Makme and Miow shout something in their language. Bobby explodes so much stuff it flies over me and hits the girls. I convulse so hard I pass a little gas. Everyone falls onto the bed to catch his or her breath.

After several minutes, the girls giggle, pick up their clothes and leave the room. Bobby moves beside me on the bed and wipes the sweat from my brow. I'm panting. What the hell did I just do?

"Not a bad start to the evening," he murmurs. I made him murmur. Good for me.

"Start?"

"Yes, Miss Thesia. That was the appetizer."

Holy shit.

Chapter 16

Lurch opens the door for me outside my apartment. I'm wearing sunglasses to shield my eyes from any sort of light. He grabs my suitcase, takes my arm, and helps me into the elevator. No words are spoken. The bell rings, and I take baby steps toward my door. Fumbling for my keys, I finally get the door open. I thank Lurch before continuing my slow steps into the apartment and back to my bedroom. Thankfully, Tease is not home.

I collapse onto my bed in a state of total shock. I don't remember the drive back from the cabin. Cabin, my ass. It's more like a giant fuck palace. Last night is a blur. After the appetizer, we went back downstairs and drank heavily for about an hour. What happened after that is hazy. I remember being back in the OBGYN office, but instead of the creepy doctor, it was Bobby dressed as one. The Asian girls were there for a few minutes, but I don't recall if they did anything to me. I do remember Bobby sitting in the chair wearing nothing but his cowboy hat. Who knows what that was about or what happened while I was passed out on the doctor's desk? What I do know is that my nipples ache, my ass feels like I spent the entire ride home sitting on a cucumber instead of a leather seat, and my cooch feels like I've given birth to a watermelon.

I strip off my clothes and inspect my body. No tattoos. That's a plus. A couple of bruises and some reddened spots, but nothing more. I don't think I'll ever drink again. I don't think I'll ever have sex again.

I crawl under the sheets, wrapping my pillow around my head. A few minutes later, the tears come. I'm not in real pain—just emotional distress. What the hell have I gotten myself into over the last few weeks? I've gone from being a lonely virgin to participating in multi-person bizarre sex marathons. That's a lot for anyone to process. When I ask myself why I've ventured down this path, the answer is always the same: Bobby Beige. He wants me to do this. He has guided me, held my hand through this truly life-changing experience. Thinking about him makes me feel better. I wish he were here to lie beside me and stroke my hair. Even though I've had enough sex to last the average person a month, I would still do him if he were here.

My iPhone makes a tweeting sound.

Text Message from BobbyB: Why are you crying? Are you okay?

Text Message from AnnisT: How do you know that?

Text Message from BobbyB: The implant is transmitting emotional distress. Are you okay?

Text Message from AnnisT: I'm fine. Why does my ass hurt?

Text Message from BobbyB: I warned you. You wouldn't listen. But you did great.

Text Message from AnnisT: Warned me about what? I don't remember much about last night.

Text Message from BobbyB: You were fucking amazing. To be such a novice, you performed like a real whore. Makme and Miow liked you too! They asked when you'd be coming back to the FRR.

Text Message from AnnisT: Am I a lesbian now?

Text Message from BobbyB: Why would you ask that?

Text Message from AnnisT: Because I enjoyed what they did to me.

Text Message from BobbyB: I enjoy it when animals lick my honey-soaked ass. Does that make me some sort of weirdo pig?

Text Message from AnnisT: Yes, it sort of does.

Text Message from BobbyB: Miss Thesia, I don't agree with labeling people. Pleasure is pleasure. I'm for all sorts of pleasure, regardless of the source.

Text Message from AnnisT: I'm not sure that's a healthy lifestyle.

Text Message from BobbyB: I make it as healthy as I can. You've seen my body.

Text Message from AnnisT: That's not what I mean. You know it. Some of the shit you're into is not normal.

Text Message from BobbyB: That may be so, but think about your life now compared to two weeks ago. Do you wish you had never shared these experiences?

He's got me. The answer is no. I'm glad to have met him, glad to walk through this crazy, screwed-up world known as Bobby Beige. I just don't know if my body and mind can keep up. He operates at a totally different level than I do. He is out of my league. Why has he chosen me? Everyone keeps telling me I'm not as good as his other women.

Text Message from BobbyB: Are you there?

Text Message from AnnisT: Yes.

Text Message from BobbyB: You know I'm right, don't you? I can't stop thinking about you, Annis. I can't wait until next weekend.

I may need that long for all my parts to recover.

Text Message from AnnisT: I look forward to it as well. I think.

Text Message from BobbyB: Get some rest. Tomorrow is a full day.

What's tomorrow? Oh, yeah. My makeover. Sleep comes easily, and Tease is the one to wake me up.

"There's some large creepy guy here to pick you up," she says.

"Oh, shit. I overslept. Tell him I'll be there in a minute."

I jump in the shower and get myself together as best as I can. Lurch hurries me down to the car, and I'm driven to an elaborate glass-enclosed building. I don't even check in. I'm taken straight to an examination room, asked to put on a paper dress, and told to sit in a reclining chair. Three doctors enter, looking down at me.

"I'm Dr. Crosby. This is Dr. Nash, and that is Dr.—"

"Stills, I get it."

"Thompson. My name is Dr. Thompson."

"Sorry," I say. I'm such a dork.

"Do you know why you are here, Miss Thesia?" asks Dr. Crosby.

"You're going to do some stuff to make me look better, I suppose."

They laugh a little, then regain their composure.

"You have a very serious friend who wants you to have a few procedures. Okay, that's an understatement. Let's just say several. Several is more than a few, right?"

"Several is a good term," says Nash.

"Yes, well, we can tell just by looking at you that there's a lot of work to do. My specialty is face, skin, and neck. Nash is our cellulite and liposuction expert. Thompson is our dentist."

Thompson examines my teeth, visibly recoiling.

"Good God, lady. Do you ever floss?"

"Yes," I lie.

"Sure you do. Sure you do."

Nash pokes at my stomach and arm fat, watching it jiggle like a metronome. "Do you exercise regularly, Miss Thesia?"

"Um. Yes."

"As often as you floss, I suppose."

And a fuck you to you too.

After more poking and prodding, Crosby delivers instructions.

"Be here at seven in the morning. No food after four tonight. Take this pill before you come to help calm your nerves. We'll get started first thing and get you home a new woman."

I nod, shake their hands, and prepare to leave—until Crosby

locks the door, turns on music, and starts unbuttoning his shirt.

"You like to party, Miss Thesia?" he asks, dancing around me.

"Um. Not really. What's going on here?"

He stops, shrugs, turns the music off, and steps back. Then, without warning, he cups my boob.

"Touch me again, and I'll kick your nuts so hard you'll be blowing semen out of your nose. Understand?

Chapter 17

The doctors—Moe, Larry, and Curly—really did a number on me. Even though I was groggy from the drugs, I'm pretty sure I got a full teeth cleaning, liposuction, lap band, manicure, pedicure, and waxing in several places. Probably another colon hydrotherapy, too—knowing Bobby.

The lipo makes me feel like I've been stabbed and beaten by a professional boxer. I haven't been able to get out of bed for two days. It's embarrassing having to use a bedpan. Tease helps, but she gags every time she takes it to the toilet. I can't eat more than a tablespoon of food—must be the lap band.

"Why did you agree to let him do this to you?" Tease keeps saying. "You were perfect the way you were. If he doesn't love you for that, fuck him. He's an asshole."

At least, that's the gist of it. And she says it constantly. Maybe she's right. But look at my new ankles! How did they do that? I can't wait to put on some sexy pumps and go out. Ankles, not kankles! And my toes—they look delicious. I feel guilty thinking about what the Asian girls would do to them in this condition.

They must have left my boobs alone. Bobby said he liked them. I'll never forget when he was lying beside me after sex, looking into my eyes. "I like your tits."

I'm excited to get on a scale. Between the procedures and not eating for days, I must have lost a lot of weight. My hair even feels different. Did they cut it while I was under? And I'm pretty sure that's the only hair left on my body. My skin is still sensitive from the waxing—especially under my armpits.

The lactation pills started working yesterday. I need to pump, but I'm too embarrassed to ask Tease. Instead, I squeeze my nips above the bedpan whenever I feel the need. It's disgusting. It doesn't make me excited about motherhood. But at least my breasts are getting bigger. There's always a silver lining.

Tweet Tweet

Text Message from BobbyB: I can't wait to see you. I'll be back in town first of next week.
Text Message from AnnisT: I feel like I've been in a car wreck.
Text Message from BobbyB: According to the doctors, you were a wreck. But they've fixed you up, my sweet Annis.
Text Message from AnnisT: Those guys were creepy. I don't like them. One of them said you asked him to 'service' me.
Text Message from BobbyB: Was that a bad idea?
Text Message from AnnisT: YES! And you will be punished as soon as I'm able to piss in a real toilet.
Text Message from BobbyB: Oh, dear. Have you been studying?
Text Message from AnnisT: Yes, and your ass is mine. Have you been self-pleasuring?

I giggle as I say that into my iPhone. I wish I had one of his asses here—one of my very own. It would make a great piece of art. I'd hang it in the living room for all my friends to admire. Dumas would never leave.

Text Message from BobbyB: I was just starting to as we were texting.
Text Message from AnnisT: Stop right now, Mister. And no sex with anyone else until I get you in the FRR.
Text Message from BobbyB: Anyone? Or anything?
Text Message from AnnisT: No orgasms. Period. If you do, I'll know, and it will be harder for you. Mommy is coming back—with a vengeance!
Text Message from BobbyB: Oh, shit. Yes, Ma'am. Are you lactating yet?

Text Message from AnnisT: Yes, and the milk is good and fresh. If you're good, maybe you can have some.

Text Message from BobbyB: Oh, yes. Yes. I'll be good. I'm so hungry. Feed me, please.

Text Message from AnnisT: That's more like it. Now, go out and buy me something expensive, or no milk for you. Mommy out!

So, the hunger games have begun. That should keep him occupied for a while. He's such a sick fuck. But if he is, what does that make me? I don't even know. I always thought I was normal. Now I'm ordering around a billionaire like he's my own little bitch. This world is insane.

By the third day, I can use the bathroom on my own—no more bedpan. That's nice. By day five, I leave the apartment to pick up a breast pump. What a relief. I must have pumped out enough for an orphanage that first day. I may feel like a cow, but I don't look like one anymore. I've lost 18 pounds, and my legs look amazing. I tried on some of Tease's sexiest shoes and actually fit inside them. Meeeeoww.

All this time at home has given me a chance to do more research on being a Dominant. I can't explain it, but my inner slut likes the idea more and more. I've got plans for Mr. Beige. Just thinking about them makes me a little wet.

Although we aren't supposed to meet until the weekend, I contact Lurch and have him take me to Beige's office. Armed with a small suitcase and a large beige raincoat, I take the express elevator to the top floor. His two big-tittied secretaries stare as I walk up.

"Hold all his calls until I come back out of that office. Push back all his appointments by an hour. Do it now, or I'll have both of you fired!"

They scramble to obey. I fling open Beige's office door, then slam it shut and lock it. His mouth drops open. "I'll call you back," he says into his headset.

"Get your ass over to the couch. Now, you little prick!"

He obeys, eyes wide with anticipation and bewilderment.

"My, my, Miss Thesia. Look at you."

"Shut the hell up. You'll speak when I tell you."

I pull out the magic marker Bobby gave me and inhale. Bobby's mouth drops open. I take another, deeper hit.

"Be careful," he whimpers. "Not too much."

My mind floods with images—buildings, planets, those goofy animals from Where the Wild Things Are, Justin Bieber, mountain bikes, yogurt machines. Holy shit, I'm dancing with the stars! Where did he get these fucking markers? A minute later, I come back to myself, sweating. I shake my head to clear it.

I set the suitcase on the coffee table and take out a riding crop. My legs spread slightly, showing off my new ankles and spiked black heels. I unbutton my raincoat, revealing black lace lingerie and my engorged breasts.

"Dear Lord," he whispers.

I slap him hard. His eyes widen, taking in my body. I can tell he likes it. Why wouldn't he? I'm as close to perfect as I'll ever be.

"Is this what you imagined, you sick fuck?"

He nods. "More so."

I strike him with the riding crop. "I said not to speak!"

I straddle him, pressing my breasts to his face. "Now, suck. Suck hard, you pathetic little man."

He does and the milk flows out so much it runs down his mouth and all over his nice shirt and ugly tie. This feels so good. I want him to keep going and going. I can tell he gets full right away but I'm not empty. "Keep sucking!"

I notice his erection beneath me. I start to dry hump him as he continues to soak himself in my breast milk. He is groaning and I am moaning. He pulls up both his hands to help massage the milk out of my breasts. Yes. That's it. Milk me like a cow. Ummm that's good.

When the milk finally starts to dry, I stand back up and look down on him. He is out of breath and his shirt is totally soaked. We may have ruined his couch.

"Stand up and turn around. Take off your pants." He does as told. His clothes are so soaked you could probably wring out a half gallon of milk. "Now the underwear. Turn around on all fours!"

"I'm so sorry. What did I do?" he says with a whimper.

"This is for your fucked up doctor friends. One of them taught me this. You better grab ahold of something."

I take out some surgical gloves and a tube of lubricant. I catch him turning around to see what I'm doing, so I slap him with the crop again. I insert my lubed glove barely into his ass and point it sideways toward his belly button.

"Relax, Bobby or this is going to be very uncomfortable."

When he releases the pressure of his sphincter, I'm able to reach in and find the prostate. I turn my fingers in a circular motion around the small triangular shaped gland. Lucky for him it feels normal. Bobby's feels very similar to the doctor's prostate when he taught me the procedure. His doctors are so messed up.

Bobby is still whimpering, but when I squeeze the gland, he screams out and semen squirts out of him onto his beige leather sofa.

"AAAAAhhUggggh," is all he can say. I pull out my hand, peel off the glove and toss it on his clean beige carpet. He has collapsed on his couch and is out of breath.

I close up my suitcase of goodies and start to button my raincoat back up. "Our arrangement has begun, Mr. Beige. Now. Where is the gift you were supposed to get for me?"

"It's downstairs in the garage. A new BMW 530d. I hope you like it. The title is in your name."

"Very well. Is there some cash in the vehicle?"

"Yes, Ma'am. A ten grand stack of $100 bills is in the glove compartment."

"If I find the car unacceptable you will be punished. If I run out of money while I'm out, you will be punished again!"

He reaches in his wallet and pulls out one of his black American Express cards and hands it to me. I didn't know they had a black one. It must be special. We'll see.

"I'll see you this weekend, Mr. Beige. Have all the staff on standby. I'm feeling…frisky."

"Yes, Ma'am."

Chapter 18

The BMW is incredible. The scent of leather fills the car, intoxicating and luxurious. The crisp stack of bills in my hand? Even better. I just try not to dwell too much on how I got them.

Okay, so I stuck my hand in a guy's ass. I wore a glove. He could have said "midget."

Life is pretty damn great right now. I look better than ever. I have a rich boyfriend. Teaching? Not for me. Today, I'm going shopping.

After changing into something more casual, my first stop is Dillard's. Time for a wardrobe upgrade and some new bags. When I arrive, I make it clear to the manager that this isn't some Pretty Woman situation where they ignore me. I have cash, I have credit, and I plan to spend—a lot. If they want my business, they'll assign me an employee to carry my bags. Otherwise, I'm taking my money to Macy's. They're quick to comply.

By the time I leave, I've charged just under eleven thousand dollars to Mr. Beige's card. He's going to have a heart attack when he sees that bill, but dresses, purses, watches, and shoes don't come cheap. And my new ankles deserve the best footwear. Serves him right for handing me over to those crazy doctors.

I splurge on perfume, lingerie, robes, towels, and sheets—the finest of everything. My new car's trunk and back seat are packed to the brim with my haul.

By the end of my spree, I'm exhausted. I've officially shopped until I dropped. I drive to The Grove, a set of townhomes I've been eyeing since college. The BMW gets me past the gate with no trouble, and the realtor informs me there's a furnished unit available for immediate rental. Perfect. I hand over two months' rent in cash, sign some papers, and get my keys.

Home sweet home. Maybe I won't move to Philadelphia after all.

After unloading and organizing my new things, I take a moment to admire the space. Three bedrooms, a spacious master bath, a gorgeous kitchen with stainless steel appliances, and a fireplace to die for. It looks brand new, like no one has ever lived here before.

When I head back to my old apartment, Tease is waiting for me.

"Why don't you answer your phone?" she asks.

"I don't know. It's new. Sometimes I don't hear it. Too many buttons." Total lie. I turned it off to avoid explaining anything to her. She's nosy, but she's also been a good friend.

"I was worried about you."

"Why?"

"Because you've been spending so much time with Beige. I don't know. There's something about him I don't like."

"Like what? It can't be his looks."

"No, but look what he asked you to do. He's flipped you like one of his foreclosed properties."

"I let him do it, Tease. And I needed it. Have you seen my new ankles?"

"Yes, yes. I've seen them. But he didn't have to make you get bigger breasts. You had nice natural ones."

I don't have the heart to tell her these are still my real boobs. She'd lose her mind over the lactation medication. Good thing I have pads on, or she'd notice me leaking. They're getting bigger every day. Can't wait to try on my new bras. My old ones are too tight.

I'm not sure how to tell Tease I'm moving out. She won't be happy. I might not even tell Bobby. Maybe I can just live here in secret. But Bobby would find me—he had that damn tracker put in my arm. He loves me, I think. Either that, or he loves weird sex. I'd like to believe it's me. Do I love him? Not sure. We've only known each other a few weeks. He's gorgeous, has a great body, and is weird as hell. But do I love him? Hell yes.

He spends time with me, spends money on me, and has sex with me. No man has ever done that for me—ever. So, love it is. I want Bobby Beige. I want him with all his quirks, his dwarfs, Asians, blimps, and all.

Tonight is study night. Time to disable the internet filter—momma is diving deep into the world of kinky porn. I'm excited to see what new discoveries I'll make.

Tweet, Tweet.

Text Message from BobbyB: I'm still in shock from your visit today.

Text Message from AnnisT: Did I give you permission to text me?

Text Message from BobbyB: No. Was that a bad idea?

Text Message from AnnisT: That's right, you little shit. You'll wait until I contact you from now on. Do not make momma angry.

Text Message from BobbyB: Yes, Ma'am.

Text Message from AnnisT: I spent a lot of your money today, and it made me cum.

I laugh as I send that one. Sometimes I crack myself up.

Text Message from BobbyB: Oh, dear.

Text Message from AnnisT: I'll be needing more. Set me up an account and get me one of those black AMEX cards with my name on it. I like that one. So do the sales clerks.

Text Message from BobbyB: Just how much spending are we talking about?

Text Message from AnnisT: Does it matter?

Text Message from BobbyB: I suppose not.

Text Message from AnnisT: Listen, baby. You go back to work and keep making money. Mommy has homework to do.

Don't disturb me.

Text Message from BobbyB: You surprise me, Miss Thesia. I'm enchanted and bewitched by you. It's hard to concentrate on work just thinking about you. I'm getting aroused just from TEXTING.

Text Message from AnnisT: Then think about baseball or whatever. No self-pleasuring. You could lose your eyesight. Now, get back to work.

Text Message from BobbyB: Alright. Beige out.

I dive into my research. The internet is a strange place. There's a group of people who get off wearing stuffed animal costumes. They call it yiffing. No skin-to-skin contact, yet they find pleasure. Okay, that's just crazy.

Then, there are those who tie their partners to massage tables and tease them for hours with feathers, riding crops, sex toys, and percussion instruments. That's erotic. I take notes.

I study spanking techniques, even warm-up stretches to prevent cramping. Helpful. I take more notes.

I find charts on "hot points" for punishment. Bobby won't like these—or maybe he will. I wonder what it'll take to make him say his safe word. How many times has he used it before? That should be my new goal. I, Annis Thesia, the Dominant, will make Bobby Beige say "midget."

My thoughts get me worked up. I need more pads.

I shut the laptop and check myself in the mirror. Holy shit, I look good. I'd fuck me. My stomach is flat, my ass is round, and I don't even see any incisions. Those doctors were weird, but they were damn good. Recovery has been surprisingly smooth.

I pat my stomach, wondering how much Bobby paid for all this. The thought makes me feel like a whore. But we have a relationship. It's unconventional, but rich men have given women gifts for centuries. I'm not a whore.

Friday arrives. I pack up my things and hit the road. The GPS guides me through Pennsylvania's country roads, its sexy male voice purring, "Turn right, Miss Thesia, just ahead."

Just for fun, I veer off course, just to hear it say, "You may want to turn around. You should turn around."

It's hot. Maybe I get why men want to fuck their cars.

Chapter 19

I'm already standing in the great room of the cabin when Bobby arrives in his blimp. I'm dressed in a tight-fitting black dress that costs more than I used to make at Lowe's in three months. The fabric feels luxurious against my skin, and I know I look good. The dress is short to showcase my new legs, and my black stilettos have tiny straps caressing my ankles. I spread my stance just past shoulder width and place both hands on my hips. My massive, milk-engorged cleavage spills from the deep V-neck of the dress, barely contained by a black lace bra. My body wants him as much as I do.

"Dear God. Look at you," he mutters. It's not quite a murmur, but it's a good start. He'll be murmuring later. He comes over, caresses me, and starts to trail his tongue along my neck. Oh my.

"I've longed for you so much. You have no idea. Let's go downstairs now. I've been so bad."

"Do you have my new little black card?"

"Yes, here. Unlimited. Take it. You can have anything, Annis. I just want you to be mine. Now. Right now."

"Settle down, sport," I whisper. "It's going to be a long night. Did you eat?"

"Yes."

"Vegetables?"

"Yes, Ma'am."

I gently stroke the back of his head as he works his magical tongue up to my earlobe, sending a warm stir through my core. I must be patient. "Alright then. Go brush your teeth and meet me down in the basement."

He kisses my cheek, grins, and runs off. When he returns, I

take him by the hand and lead him to the elevator. I stop at the door.

"Before we go in there, I want you to know this is for my pleasure as well as yours."

"Give it to me, give it to me."

"Although what I mean to do to you is demeaning in every way, shape, and form, I want you to understand it is not my intention to actually demean you."

"Yes, demean me. D'fucking mean me, Mommy."

The elevator dings, and the doors slide open. Bobby's eyes widen with excitement. I have spent the last week working with the staff and Lurch to transform the western town into a whimsical amusement park. The OBGYN is now a pediatrician's office. The bar has become an ice cream parlor. The stable is a haunted house, and in the middle of the street, a small carousel spins beneath twinkling lights. The Asian massage parlor remains unchanged—I can see Makme and Miow moving inside.

"How did you do this?" Bobby asks, taking it all in.

"Lurch and I wanted to surprise you. Now, go see the doctor and change into something more appropriate, dear. I'll meet you at the carousel in twenty minutes."

"I can't wait!"

He has no idea the doctor will be running a full battery of tests on him—prostate exam, urine test, stool test, semen analysis, and a handful of injections. I even paid extra for the doctor to be as rude and insulting as possible. He should emerge in a very foul mood.

I stroll into the Asian Palace, where my new friends are waiting.

"Hello, Miss Thesia. We've been talking about you."

"I want a pedicure from Makme and a scalp massage from Miow. You will not call me Miss Thesia. Tonight, I am Domino."

"Yes, Miss Domeeeno."

"Not domeen-no. Do-men-no. Domino. Got it?"

They nod instead of trying to say it again.

Domino isn't the most intimidating name, but it's the closest I could get to 'Dominant.' Annis the Dominant just doesn't have the same ring. But I have to remember—this is a fantasy.

Even though I'm just getting a massage and pedicure, these two turn it into some sort of sensual game. Makme soaks my feet, her tiny fingers slipping between my toes as she makes little breathy sounds, as if I'm hurting her just a bit. Miow drags her fingertips through my hair, then traces her nails lightly over my neck, moaning softly as she does. It awakens something primal in me, and I have to close my eyes to keep my mind from wandering too far.

When I hear Bobby is done, I shake off the lingering thoughts and step out of the massage chair.

"I'll be out in a minute, Sweety!"

"The doctor hurt me, Mommy. He's a bad man!"

"Just give me a moment!"

"He poked me over and over! And then he stuck a water hose up my butt!"

The Asian girls giggle. I do too, but I can't break character. "Remember, ladies. Meet me in the dungeon in an hour."

"Yes, Miss Domeeeno."

I open the door, and Bobby collapses at my waist, hugging me. He's dressed in a brightly colored shirt and shorts combo, white socks, and white shoes. A silly child's hat with a propeller sits atop his head, and a pacifier dangles from a lanyard around his neck.

"I'm hungry, Mommy. I'm really hungry."

I know what he wants, and it's time. I lead him to a park bench, where he eagerly slides the spaghetti strap of my dress down and unclasps my front-access bra. As he curls into my lap, I suddenly feel a surge of sympathy for mothers who are shamed for breastfeeding in public. It's just a natural part of life. What's the big deal?

Bobby must have been starving. He drains one side completely and doesn't slow until the other is halfway empty. When he stops, I wipe the milk from his chin and pat his back. Instead of burping, he suddenly vomits all over the sidewalk.

Whoa. Definitely not kissing him until he cleans up.

"Does Bobby feel better now?" I coo. "I bet you do."

He looks up at me, pale as a ghost. I clean his chin again and escort him to the carousel, helping him onto a horse. He manages a weak smile.

I start the carousel at level one, watching as the horse glides up and down. The bells and music are bright and nostalgic.

"Weeee, look at you, Bobby!" I call as he goes by.

"Weeeee!" he manages to say.

I crank it to level three. The speed forces Bobby to grip the pole tightly, his golden hair whipping in the wind. Even in his ridiculous outfit, he looks sexy.

Level five. Centrifugal force lifts him off the horse, his legs flailing sideways as he clings to the pole. As he whirls past, I hear the faint sound of "Mid..." and then a "Git."

I slam the red STOP button. The ride jerks to a halt, launching Bobby down the street, where he tumbles in a heap. His legs are scraped and bleeding onto his pristine white socks, and a fresh cut mars his perfect forehead.

"Did you say 'midget'?"

"No...Mommy. But, shit, that hurt."

"Well, then get up. If you can walk, you can fuck."

"Yes, Ma'am."

"Do you want some ice cream, Sweety?"

"I don't think so. My tummy hurts."

"Alright, dear. Come with me."

I lead Bobby down the street and into what used to be the saloon. Tonight, it's a grand castle, complete with armored guards. A small dwarf in a jester's outfit skips past, bells jingling, shooting me a glare.

"What is this place?" Bobby asks in awe.

"This...is for people who behave, Bobby. But you...you're going downstairs."

"Downstairs? There is no downstairs."

"That's where you're wrong."

The guards open a door, revealing a torch-lit stone staircase descending into darkness.

"It looks scary," Bobby whispers.

"It should. Now get the hell down there."

Chapter 20

At the bottom of the steps, Bobby realizes things have just become a lot more serious. The room is an exact replica of a medieval dungeon, with the exception of a leather couch, a massage table, a birthing chair, and a full mascot costume of the Pittsburgh Parrot.

Bobby turns to me and says, "You have made me so happy. You are amazing."

I smile and clap my hands. Makme and Miow enter the torture room and begin tying Bobby to straps that will hold him against the wall. I step away to change into something more appropriate.

"Away from him!" I shout at the two Asian girls a few minutes later. I walk back in carrying a short whip, wearing a suit of leather so tight it looks like I was dipped in it. My heels are six inches tall, and a black mask covers my eyes. I step up, inches from Bobby Beige. The girls have stripped him of all his clothes, and the torchlight flickers off his shiny skin. He looks glorious. I cross my eyes beneath the mask.

"Jeez, don't do that. Please. I'll be good."

I run my hands down his stomach, caressing his hips. Bending down as if I'm going to take him in my mouth, I stop just short. A move I learned from my roommate. Instead, I continue to touch him all around except where he wants it most. It doesn't take long before he is fully aroused.

"There it is!" I say, smacking it on the head with my palm. Taking eight steps back, I reach into my suitcase of goodies and pull out a pair of iron horseshoes. I clink them together, just like I did as a child to knock the sand off before throwing them.

"Hold on a minute," Bobby says.

"Silence! Be very still."

"I'm tied up by all fours! Being still is not optional! What the fuck are you doing?"

I flip the first horseshoe at him. He grimaces as it hits him full on the chest and falls to the floor. CLANK CLANK.

"Shit, Annis. That hurt!"

"Pain is good! It lets you know you're alive! Remember?"

The second horseshoe goes a little lower and bounces off his erection. No ringer, but I'm getting closer. Bobby groans.

"Please stop. This could cause some serious damage!"

"But, it's not one of your hard limits, Bobby. You have a safe word. Let's hear it."

He grimaces but says nothing until the third horseshoe is on its way. This one hits his stomach and slides down, coming to rest on his impressive length.

"Ringer!" I shout. The Asian girls clap their hands, congratulating me.

"Come, girls. You give it a try. Don't lose your concentration, Bobby!"

"No. Please!" Bobby mutters. We've already got him muttering.

Makme picks up the horseshoes and steps back. She wildly flings one, and it makes a loud THUNK as it hits Bobby in the face.

"Whoops. Too high, Makme. Try again."

She never lands a ringer. All she does is hit Bobby in the chest, leg, and foot. But, to her credit, never once in the balls. Miow doesn't do any better. When Bobby finally loses his arousal, we stop the game. What's the point anymore?

"Looks like Mr. Beige has lost interest," I say. Clapping my hands, Makme brings me a high-end Oreck vacuum cleaner. We've installed a special attachment just for Bobby.

"What the hell now?" he says.

"Seems like you need a little pumping action. You're getting a little soft."

"Hey. I've read about this, and I want you to seriously reconsider. This type of thing is not safe. The rules say you can't—"

The tube is placed around his manhood, and the vacuum is turned on. I thought I had seen Bobby's eyes widen before, but never like this. It is total terror. I turn it off after only a few seconds. He's already gasping for breath.

"Stop. HUFF Please. Not cool. Don't—HUFF—continue. HUFF…"

I place the tip of the vacuum hose on his nipple, then turn it on.

"AAAAAAHHHHHHH!" I turn it off.

"Well. Well. This is what it's like to have some rich billionaire suck on your tits for milk. How do you like it, Bobby?"

"Don't. Okay. We can stop the lactation…" I turn it on, sucking on the other nipple.

"AHHHHHHHH. SHIT! STOP! MIDGET! MIDGET!" I turn it off.

"Wow! The safe word. And so soon in the evening. You pussy."

His heavy breathing continues. I look down on the floor. Bobby has pissed.

"I thought peeing was a hard limit, Bobby!"

"Voluntary, you bitch. The contract prohibited voluntary urination. Does this look voluntary to you?"

I slap his face, hard. Then I grab both his testicles and squeeze. His mouth opens.

"Bitch? You called me… a bitch?" I squeeze tighter, and he whimpers.

"I'm sorry. It was a mistake. Please. Forget I said that. You're not a bitch. You are an exceptional woman."

"Then you better do as I say and not back sass."

I let him go, and he regains his breath. Makme and Miow

undo his straps, and he collapses to his knees. We spread oil all over his bruised body and force him into the Pittsburgh Parrot costume.

I grew up watching Pirate games at the stadium and loved the Pittsburgh Parrot. He was hilarious. Once Bobby is secure inside, we bring down the dwarf.

"Is the money already transferred to my account?" he asks, looking up.

I show him the receipt.

"Alright, let's do this."

"Who is that speaking out there?" Bobby asks. He can't see out of the costume because we plugged up the eyeholes. The dwarf strips and oils himself. The Asian girls offer to help, but he refuses. I'm shocked at the size of his pork sword. He puts on a small holster belt with several sex toys attached. We unzip the Parrot costume, and in he crawls.

Bobby screams. The parrot costume falls to the dungeon floor and rolls around. Bumps and bulges expand inside as the fight unfolds. Eventually, the struggle stops. Bobby murmurs softly from inside.

"Midget."

I ring the bell, and Makme unzips the back of the parrot outfit. The dwarf spills out, slimy and drenched in sweat, like the parrot just gave birth. He stands up, shoots me another fuck you, lady look, and towels off.

"Nice work," I tell him.

"Your boy was difficult, but I calmed him down. He won't be forgetting this little episode anytime soon. You can call me again, but the price will be double. He vacated his bladder in there, and I won't be involved in anything like that again."

"I understand. Thanks for your help."

"Kiss my ass, lady."

He's an angry elf, I think to myself.

I turn to the staff. "Get him bathed and cleaned up before

sending him upstairs to me."

"Yes, Miss Domeeeno."

An hour later, I'm sitting in the great room of the cabin, sipping some of Bobby's best wine. The moon is bright, reflecting off the blimp outside. Bobby gingerly walks in and takes a seat beside me on the couch.

"I may have underestimated you," he says between groans.

"There is no 'may' to it. You did. You made me do things I didn't want to do. You had me take stupid pills to produce breast milk. You insulted me repeatedly without so much as an apology. And so have your doctors and staff. Just because you're rich doesn't mean you know everything. You don't know shit."

"You may be right. I do not know the shit."

"This was my goodbye gift to you, Bobby. I wanted to prove I could make you say the safe word, and I did. Twice in one night. Now, we're done."

"But, Annis. No, please no. Look at where you have taken me! This is the most amazing night of my life. No one has ever done this to me before. You have a true talent. I must have you stay with me. Please! I beg you!"

His eyes are genuinely teary. I think he cares for me, but he's batshit crazy. This relationship is too dysfunctional to work. I just want to be a teacher. Hell, I'll even give him back his stuff if he wants. But he'll have to file a lawsuit first. He probably will. He can be a real cheapskate.

He rests his head in my lap, and I gently run my fingers through his hair. With everything that just happened, I completely forgot to have actual sex. Now it feels too awkward. I'm in the middle of telling him it's over—But would you fuck me real quick before I go? That sounds like something a guy would say. I can't do that.

I finish my wine and head for the door.

"You shouldn't drive after drinking."

"I had one glass, Bobby. I'll be fine. Plus, I had some crackers, so it wasn't on an empty stomach."

"Oh, well. Then I suppose this is goodbye, Miss Thesia."

Not exactly the grand farewell I was looking for, but for Bobby, that's about as romantic as it gets. The BMW dings as I stand there, looking at his pretty eyes. He licks his lips and puckers at me. I cross my eyes at him, then climb into the car.

The drive back to Pittsburgh is peaceful. I reflect on my time with Bobby Beige, the billionaire. I've learned so much in such a short time. Will it make me a better woman? Who knows? What will life be like with the next man I meet? Compared to Bobby, the relationship might seem stale and boring. The next man to date Annis Thesia is going to have his hands full, that's for sure. And not just with engorged breasts.

Tweet, Tweet.

Text Message from BobbyB: We totally forgot to fuck. Get back here, and I'll make it worth your while.
Text Message from AnnisT: Alright, be there in an hour.

The End of Book One

Book Two is "Fifty Shades of Marker," and continues the exploits of Annis and Bobby.

Epilogue

This is your assignment.

If you are listening on Audible, post a review. The Audible version only came out in 2025. I need reviews.

Post something on X, Instagram, or BookTok about this. I don't care what you say, but post something.

www.reidmockery.com

Also by Reid Mockery

Fourth Wing Parody: Fifth Wing
The Housemaid Parody: The Horsemaid
Where The Crawdads Sh*t
Divergent Parody: Detergent
Fifty Shades of Beige Trilogy
The Fault is All Yours

Printed in Dunstable, United Kingdom